Arabel's Raven

Other Harcourt Books by Joan Aiken

JOAN AIKEN

Arabel's Raven

Illustrated by
Quentin Blake

An Odyssey Classic
Harcourt, Inc.
Orlando Austin New York San Diego London

www.HarcourtBooks.com

First published by Doubleday & Company, Inc., 1974
First Odyssey Classics edition 2007

Library of Congress Cataloging-in-Publication Data
Aiken, Joan, 1924–2004.
Arabel's raven/by Joan Aiken; illustrated by Quentin Blake.
v.   cm.
Summary: Presents three previously published works
about a pet raven named Mortimer, who talks, eats everything
in sight, and causes all sorts of trouble.
Contents: Arabel's raven—The bread bin—The escaped black mamba
and other things. [1. Ravens—Fiction.   2. Birds as pets—Fiction.
3. Humorous stories.]   I. Blake, Quentin, ill.   II. Title.
PZ7.A2695Arb   2007
[Fic]—dc22   2006102553
ISBN 978-0-15-206094-7

Text set in Bodoni
Designed by Cathy Riggs

A C E G H F D B

Printed in the United States of America

CONTENTS

Arabel's Raven

Arabel's Raven

On a stormy night in March, not long ago, a respectable taxi driver named Ebenezer Jones found himself driving home, very late, through the somewhat wild and sinister district of London known as Rumbury Town. Mr. Jones had left Rumbury Tube Station behind him, and was passing the long, desolate piece of land called Rumbury Waste, when, in the street not far ahead, he observed a large, dark, upright object. It was rather smaller than a coal scuttle, but bigger than a quart cider bottle, and it was moving slowly from one side of the street to the other.

Mr. Jones had approached to within about twenty yards of this object when a motorcycle with two riders shot by him, going at a reckless pace and cutting in very close. Mr. Jones braked sharply, looking in his rearview mirror. When he looked forward again he saw that the motorcycle must have struck the upright object in passing, for it was now lying on its side, just ahead of his front wheels.

He brought his taxi to a halt.

"Not but what I daresay I'm being foolish," he thought. "There's plenty in this part of town that's best left alone. But you can't see something like that happen without stopping to have a look."

He got out of his cab.

What he found in the road was a large black bird, almost two feet long, with a hairy fringe around its beak. At first he thought it was dead. At his approach, however, it slightly opened one eye, then shut it again.

"Poor thing; it's probably stunned," thought Mr. Jones.

His horoscope in the *Hackney Drivers' Herald* that morning had said: "Due to your skill a life will be saved today." Mr. Jones had been worrying slightly, as he drove homeward, because up till now he had not, so far as he knew, saved any lives that day, except by avoiding pedestrians however recklessly they walked into the road without looking.

"This'll be the life I'm due to save," he thought, "must be, for it's five to midnight now." And he went back to his cab for the bottle of brandy and teaspoon he always carried in the toolbox in case lady passengers turned faint.

It is not so easy as you might believe to give brandy to a large bird lying unconscious in the street. After five minutes there was a good deal of brandy on the cobblestones, and some up Mr. Jones's sleeve, and some in his shoes, but he could not be sure that any had actually gone down the bird's throat. The difficulty was that he needed at least three hands: one to hold the bottle, and one to hold the spoon, and one to hold the bird's beak open. If he prized open the beak with the handle of the teaspoon, it was sure to shut again before he had time to reverse the spoon and tip in some brandy.

A hand fell on his shoulder.

"Just what do you think you're doing?" inquired one of two policemen (they always traveled in pairs through Rumbury Town) who had left their van and were standing over him.

The other policeman sniffed in a disapproving manner.

Mr. Jones straightened slowly.

"I was just giving some brandy to this rook," he explained. He was rather embarrassed, because he had spilled such a lot of the brandy.

"Rook? That's no rook," said the officer who had sniffed. "That's a raven. Look at its hairy beak."

"Whatever it is, it's stunned," said Mr. Jones. "A motorcycle hit it."

"Ah," said the second officer, "that'll have been one of the pair who just pinched thirty thousand quid from Lloyds Bank in the High Street. It's the Cash-and-Carat boys—the ones who've done a lot of burglaries around here lately. Did you see which way they went?"

"No," said Mr. Jones, tipping up the raven's head, "but they'll have a dent on their motorcycle. Could one of you hold the bottle for me?"

"You don't want to give him brandy. Hot sweet tea's what you want to give him."

"That's right," said the other policeman. "And an ice pack under the back of his neck."

"Burn feathers in front of his beak."

"Slap his hands."

"Undo his shoelaces."

"Put him in the fridge."

"He hasn't got any shoelaces," said Mr. Jones, not best pleased at all this advice. "If you aren't going to hold the bottle, why don't you go on and catch the blokes that knocked him over?"

"Oh, *they*'ll be well away by now. Besides, they carry guns. We'll go back to the station," said the first policeman. "And you'd best not stay here, giving intoxicating liquor to a bird, or we might have to take you in for loitering in a suspicious manner."

"I can't just leave the bird here in the road," said Mr. Jones.

"Take it with you, then."

"Can't you take it to the station?"

"Not likely," said the second policeman. "No facilities for ravens there."

They stood with folded arms, watching, while Mr. Jones slowly picked up the bird (it weighed about as much as a fox terrier) and put it in his taxi. And they were still watching (he saw them in his rearview mirror) as he started up and drove off.

So that was how Mr. Jones happened to take the raven back with him to Number Six, Rainwater Crescent, London N.W. 3½, on a windy March night.

When he got home, nobody was up, which was not surprising, since it was after midnight.

He would have liked to wake his daughter, Arabel, who was fond of birds and animals. But since she was quite young—not yet school age—he thought he had better not. And he knew he must not wake his wife, Martha, who had to be at work, at Round & Round, the record shop in the High Street, at nine in the morning.

He laid the raven on the kitchen floor, opened the window to give it air, put on the kettle for hot sweet tea, and, while he had the match lighted, burned a feather duster under the raven's beak. Nothing happened, except that the smoke made Mr. Jones cough. And he saw no way of slapping the raven's hands or undoing its shoelaces, so he took some ice cubes and a jug of milk from the fridge. He left the fridge door open because his hands were full, and anyway, it would slowly swing shut by itself.

With great care he slid a little row of ice cubes under the back of the raven's neck.

The kettle boiled and he made the tea: a spoonful for each person and one for the pot, three in all. He also spread himself a slice of bread and fish spread because he didn't see why he shouldn't have a little something as well as the bird. He poured out a cup of tea for himself and an eggcupful for the raven, putting plenty of sugar in both.

But when he turned around, eggcup in hand, the raven was gone.

"Bless me," Mr. Jones said. "There's ingratitude for you! After all my trouble! I suppose he flew out the window; those ice cubes certainly did the trick quick. I wonder if it would be a good notion to carry some ice cubes with me in the cab? I could put them in a vacuum flask—might be better than brandy if lady passengers turn faint..."

Thinking these thoughts he finished his tea (and the raven's; no sense in leaving it to get cold), turned out the light, and went to bed.

In the middle of the night he thought, "Did I put the milk back in the fridge?"

And he thought, "No, I didn't."

And he thought, "I ought to get up and put it away."

And he thought, "It's a cold night, the milk's not going to turn between now and breakfast. Besides, Thursday tomorrow, it's my early day."

So he rolled over and went to sleep.

Every Thursday Mr. Jones drove the local fish-monger, Mr. Finney, over to Colchester to buy oysters at five in the morning. So, next day, up he got, off he went. Made himself a cup of tea, finished the milk in the jug, never looked in the fridge.

An hour after he had gone (which was still very early), Mrs. Jones got up in her turn and put on the kettle. Finding the milk jug empty she went yawning to the fridge and pulled the door open, failing to notice that it had been prevented from shutting properly by the handle of a burnt feather duster which had fallen against the hinge. But she noticed what was inside the fridge all right. She let out a shriek that brought Arabel running downstairs.

Arabel was little and fair. She had gray eyes and at the moment she was wearing a white nightdress that made her look like a lampshade with two feet sticking out from the bottom. One of the feet had a blue sock on.

"What's the matter, Ma?" she said.

"There's a great awful *bird* in the fridge!" sobbed Mrs. Jones. "And it's eaten all the cheese and a black currant tart and five pints of milk and a bowl of drippings and a pound of sausages. All that's left is the lettuce."

"Then we'll have lettuce for breakfast," said Arabel. But Mrs. Jones said she didn't fancy lettuce that had spent the night in the fridge with a great awful bird.

"And how are we going to get it out of there?"

"The lettuce?"

"The *bird*!" said Mrs. Jones, switching off the kettle and pouring hot water into a pot without any tea in it.

Arabel opened the fridge door, which had swung shut. There sat the bird, among the empty milk bottles, but he was a lot bigger than they were. There was a certain amount of wreckage around him—torn foil, and cheese wrappings, and milk splashes, and bits of pastry, and crumbs of drippings, and rejected lettuce leaves. It was like Rumbury Waste after a Sunday picnic.

Arabel looked at the raven, and he looked back at her.

"His name's Mortimer," she said.

"No it's not, no it's not!" cried Mrs. Jones, taking a loaf from the bread bin and absentmindedly running the tap over it. "We said you could have a hamster when you were five, or a puppy or a kitten when you were six, and of course call it what you wish. Oh my *stars*, look at that creature's toenails, if nails they can be called, but not a bird like that, a great hairy awful thing eating us out of house and home, as big as a fire extinguisher and all the color of a charcoal biscuit—"

But Arabel was looking at the raven and he was looking back at her.

"His name's Mortimer," she said. And she put both arms around the raven, not an easy thing to do, all jammed in among the milk bottles as he was, and lifted him out.

"He's very heavy," she said, and set him down on the kitchen floor.

"So I should think, considering he's got a pound of sausages, a bowl of drippings, five pints of milk, half a pound of New Zealand cheddar, and a black currant tart inside him," said Mrs. Jones. "I'll open the window. Perhaps he'll fly out."

She opened the window. But Mortimer did not fly out. He was busy examining everything in the kitchen very thoroughly. He tapped the table legs with his beak—they were metal and clinked. Then he took everything out of the garbage bin—a pound of peanut shells, two Pepsi cans, and some jam tart cases. He particularly liked the jam tart cases, which he pushed under the linoleum. Then he walked over to the fireplace—it was an old-fashioned kitchen— and began chipping out the mortar from between the

bricks. Mrs. Jones had been gazing at the raven as if she were under a spell, but when he began on the fireplace, she said, "*Don't* let him do that!"

"Mortimer," said Arabel, "we'd like you not to do that, please."

Mortimer turned his head right around on its black feathery neck and gave Arabel a thoughtful, considering look. Then he made his first remark, which was a deep croak, hoarse and rasping: "Kaarrk."

It said, plain as words: "Well, all right, I won't do it *this* time, but I make no promise that I won't do it some time. And I think you are being unreasonable."

"Wouldn't you like to see the rest of the house, Mortimer?" said Arabel. And she held open the kitchen door. Mortimer walked—he never hopped—very slowly through, into the hall and looked at the stairs. They seemed to interest him greatly. He began going up them hand over hand—or, rather, beak over claw.

When he was halfway up, the telephone rang. It stood on the windowsill at the foot of the stairs, and Mortimer watched as Mrs. Jones came to answer it.

Mr. Jones was ringing from Colchester to ask if his wife wanted any oysters.

"Oysters!" she said. "That bird you left in the fridge has eaten sausages, cheese, drippings, black currant tart, drunk five pints of milk, now he's chewing the stairs, and you ask if I want oysters? Perhaps I should feed him caviar as well?"

"Bird I left in the fridge?" Mr. Jones was puzzled. "What bird, Martha?"

"That great black crow, or whatever it is. Arabel calls it Mortimer and she's leading it all over the house, and now it's taken all the spools of thread from my sewing drawer and is pushing them under the doormat."

"Not *it*, Ma. *He*. Mortimer," said Arabel, going to open the front door and take the letters from the mailman. But Mortimer got there first and received the letters in his beak.

The mailman was so startled that he dropped his whole sack of mail in a puddle and gasped, "Nevermore will I stay later than half past ten at the Oddfellows Ball or touch a drop stronger than Caribbean lemon, *nevermore!*"

"Nevermore," said Mortimer, pushing two bills and a postcard under the doormat. Then he retrieved the postcard again by spearing it clean through the middle. Mrs. Jones let out a wail.

"Arabel, *will* you come in out of the street in your nightie! Look what that bird's done, chewing up the gas bill. Nevermore, indeed! I should just about say it *was* nevermore. No, I don't want any oysters, which bring me out in raised red irritations and hiccups as you know, Ebenezer Jones, and always have, and please shut the front door, and *stop* that bird from pushing all those plastic flowers under the stair carpet."

Mr. Jones could make nothing of all this, so he hung up. Five minutes later the telephone rang again. This time it was Mrs. Jones's sister Brenda, to ask if Martha would like to come to a bingo drive that evening, but Mortimer got there first; he picked up the receiver with his claw, exactly as he had seen Mrs. Jones do, delivered a loud clicking noise into it—*click*—and said, "Nevermore!"

Then he replaced the receiver.

"My lord!" Brenda said to her husband. "Ben and Martha must have had a terrible quarrel; he answered the phone and he didn't sound a *bit* like himself!"

Meanwhile, Mortimer had climbed upstairs and was in the bathroom trying the faucets; it took him less than five minutes to work out how to turn them on. He liked to watch the cold water running, but the hot, with its clouds of steam, for some reason annoyed him, and he began throwing things at the hot faucets: bits of soap, sponges, nail brushes, facecloths.

They choked up the plughole and presently there was a flood.

"Mortimer, I think you'd better not stay in the bathroom," Arabel said.

Mortimer was good at giving people black looks; now he gave Arabel one. But she had a red wagon, which had once been filled with wooden building blocks. The blocks had long ago been scattered and lost, but the wagon was in good repair.

"Mortimer, wouldn't you like a ride in this red wagon?"

Mortimer thought he would. He climbed into the wagon and stood there, waiting.

When Mrs. Jones discovered Arabel pulling Mortimer along in the wagon she nearly had a fit.

"It's not bad enough that you've adopted that big, ugly, sulky bird, but you have to pull him along in a *wagon?* Don't his legs work? Why can't he walk, may I ask?"

"He doesn't feel like walking just now," Arabel said.

"Of course! And I suppose he's *forgotten* how to *fly?*"

"I like pulling him in the wagon," Arabel said, and she pulled him into the garden. Presently Mrs. Jones went off to work at Round & Round, the record shop, and Granny came in to look after Arabel. All Granny ever did was sit and knit. She didn't mind answering the phone, but every time it rang Mortimer got there first, picked up the receiver, and said, "Nevermore!"

People who had called up for a taxi were puzzled and said to one another, "Mr. Jones must have retired."

Lunch was baked beans. Mortimer enjoyed the baked beans, but his table manners were very lighthearted. He liked knocking spoons and forks off the table, pushing them under the sisal matting, and fetching them out again with a lot of excitement. Granny wasn't so keen on this.

While Granny was having her nap Arabel looked at the funnies and Mortimer looked at the stairs. There seemed to be something about stairs that appealed to him.

When Mr. Jones came home at teatime the first thing he said was: "What's happened to the three bottom steps?"

"What has, then?" Granny was shortsighted and anyway busy spreading jam.

"They aren't there."

"It wasn't Mortimer's fault," said Arabel. "He didn't know we need the stairs."

"Mortimer? Who's Mortimer?"

Just then Mrs. Jones came home.

"That bird has got to go," said Mr. Jones the minute she had put down her shopping basket and taken off her coat.

"Who's talking? *You* were the one who left him in the fridge."

Mortimer looked morose and sulky at Mr. Jones's words. He sank his head between his shoulders and ruffled up the beard around his beak and turned his toes in, as if he did not care one way or the other. But Arabel went so white that her father thought she was going to faint.

"If Mortimer goes," she said, "I shall cry *all* the time. Very likely I shall die!"

"Oh well...," said Mr. Jones. "But mind, if he stays, he's not to eat any more stairs!"

Just the same, during the next week or so, Mortimer did chew up six more stairs. The family had to go to bed by climbing a ladder. Luckily it was an aluminum fruit ladder, or Mortimer would probably have chewed it up, too; he was very fond of timber.

There was a bit of trouble because he wanted to sleep in the fridge at night, but Mrs. Jones put a stop to that; in the end he agreed to sleep in the bathroom cupboard. Then there was a bit more trouble because he pushed all the soap and toothbrushes under the bathroom linoleum; they had to get in the fire brigade to climb through the window, as the bathroom door wouldn't open.

"He's not to be left alone in the house," Mr. Jones said. "On the days when Arabel goes to play group, Martha, he'll have to go to work with you."

"Why can't he come to play group with me?" Arabel asked.

Mr. Jones just laughed at that question.

Mrs. Jones was not enthusiastic about taking Mortimer to work with her.

"So I'm to pull him up the High Street in that red wagon? You must be joking."

"He can ride on your shopping bag on wheels," Arabel said. "He'll like that."

At first the owners of the record shop, Mr. Round and Mr. Toby Round, were quite pleased to have Mortimer sitting on the counter. People who lived in Rumbury Town heard about the raven; they came in out of curiosity, and then they played records, and then, as often as not, bought them. And at first Mortimer was so astonished at the music that he sat still on the counter for hours at a time looking like a stuffed bird. At teatime, when Arabel came home from play group, she told him what she had been doing and pulled him around in the red wagon.

Several other shops in Rumbury Town were burgled: Brown's the ironmongers, and Mr. Finney the fishmonger, and the Tutti-Frutti Candy Shoppe.

Mr. Jones found a carpenter who said he would come along on Sunday and mend the stairs.

Everything seemed to be going all right.

But presently Mortimer began to be bored by just sitting listening to music. There was a telephone on the counter. One day when it rang Mrs. Jones was wrapping up a record for a customer, so Mortimer got there first.

"Can you tell me the name of the new Weevils' LP?" said a voice.

"Nevermore!" said Mortimer.

Also Mortimer began taking triangular bites out of the edges of records. After that it wasn't so easy to sell them. Then he noticed the spiral stairs which led down to the classic and folk departments. One morning Mr. Round and Mr. Toby Round and Mrs. Jones were all very busy arranging a display of new issues in the shop window; when they had finished they discovered that Mortimer had eaten the spiral staircase.

"Mrs. Jones, you and your bird will have to go. We have kind, long-suffering natures, but Mortimer has done eight hundred and seventeen pounds, seventy-two pence' worth of damage; you may have a year to repay it. Please don't trouble to come in for the rest of the week."

"Glad I am *I* haven't such a kind, long-suffering nature," snapped Mrs. Jones, and she dumped Mortimer on top of her wheeled shopping bag and dragged him home. "Stairs!" she said to Arabel. "What's the use of a bird who eats stairs? Gracious knows there's enough rubbish in the world—why can't he eat soda bottles, or ice-cream cartons, or used cars, or oil slicks, tell me that? But no! He

has to eat the only thing that joins the upstairs to the downstairs."

"Nevermore," said Mortimer.

"Tell that to the space cavalry!" said Mrs. Jones.

Arabel and Mortimer went and sat side by side on the bottom rung of the fruit ladder leaning against one another and very quiet.

"When I'm grown up," Arabel said to Mortimer, "we'll live in a house with a hundred stairs and you can eat them all."

Next day Mrs. Jones found another job, at Peter Stone, the jeweler's, in the High Street. She had to take both Arabel and Mortimer with her to work, since play group was finished until after Easter, and Granny had gone to Southend on a visit. Arabel pulled Mortimer to the shop every day in the red wagon. Peter Stone, the jeweler, had no objections.

"The more people in the shop, the less chance of a holdup," he said. "Too much we're hearing about these Cash-and-Carat boys for my taste. Raided the supermarket yesterday, they did; took two thousand cans of best Jamaica blend coffee, as the cash register was jammed. Coffee? What would they want with two thousand cans?"

"Perhaps they were thirsty," Arabel said. She and Mortimer were looking at their reflections in a glass case full of bracelets. Mortimer tapped the glass in an experimental way with his beak.

"That bird, now," Peter Stone said, giving Mortimer a thoughtful look. "He'll behave himself? He won't go swallowing any diamonds? The brooch he's looking at now is worth forty thousand pounds."

Mrs. Jones drew herself up. "Behave himself? Naturally he'll behave himself," she said. "Any diamonds he swallows I guarantee to replace!"

A police sergeant came into the shop. "I've a message for your husband," he said to Mrs. Jones. "We've found a motorcycle, and we'd be glad if he'd step up to the station and say if he can identify it as the one that passed him the night the bank was robbed." Then he saw Mortimer. "Is that the bird that got knocked over? *He'd* better come along as well; we can see if he fits the dent in the gas tank."

"Nevermore," said Mortimer, who was eyeing a large gold clock. But it was under a glass dome.

"He'd better not talk like that to the super," the sergeant said, "or he'll be charged with obstructing the police."

"Have they got any theories about the identity of the gang?" Peter Stone asked.

"No, they always wear masks. But we're pretty sure they're locals and have a hideout somewhere in the district, because we always lose track of them so fast. One odd feature is that they have a small accomplice, about the size of that bird there," the sergeant said, giving Mortimer a hard stare.

"How do you know?"

"When they robbed the supermarket, someone got in through the manager's cat door and opened a window from inside. If birds had fingerprints," the sergeant said, "I wouldn't mind taking the prints of that shifty-looking fowl. *He* could get through a cat flap, easy enough."

"Kaaark," said Mortimer.

"Your opinions are uncalled for," said Mrs. Jones. "Thoughtless our Mortimer may be, untidy at times, but honest as a Bath bun, I'll have you know. And the night the supermarket was robbed he was in our bathroom cupboard with his head tucked under his wing."

"I've known some Bath buns not all they should be," said the sergeant.

Five minutes after the sergeant had gone, Peter Stone went off for his lunch.

And five minutes after *that*, two masked men walked into the shop.

One of them pointed a gun at Mrs. Jones and Arabel, the other smashed a glass case and took out the diamond brooch which Peter Stone had said was worth forty thousand pounds.

Out of the gunman's pocket clambered a gray squirrel with an extremely villainous expression, which looked hopefully around.

"Nothing for you to do here, Sam," said the masked man who had taken the diamond. "Piece of apple pie, this job."

The squirrel seemed disappointed, but the man with the gun said, "Don't be so stupid. Give Sam the brooch and he can use the bird; ha ha, he can hitch a ride to our snuggery. I've a score to settle with that bird, anyway."

Mortimer, who was eating one of the cheese sandwiches Mrs. Jones had brought for her lunch, suddenly found a gun jammed against his ribs. The squirrel jumped on his back.

"You'd better cooperate, coal face," the gunman said. "This is a flyjack. Fly where Sam tells you, or you'll be blown to forty bits. Sam carries a bomb around his neck on a shoelace; all he has to do is pull out the pin with his teeth."

"Oh, please don't blow up Mortimer," Arabel said to the gunman. "I think he's forgotten how to fly."

"He'd better remember pretty fast."

"Oh dear, Mortimer, perhaps you'd better do what they say."

With a croak that could be heard all over the jeweler's shop, Mortimer unfolded his wings and, to his own surprise as much as anyone else's, flew out through the open door with Sam sitting on his back. The two thieves walked calmly after him.

As soon as they were gone, Mrs. Jones went into hysterics, and Arabel rang the alarm buzzer.

In no time a police car bounced to a stop outside, with siren screaming and lights flashing. Peter Stone came rushing back from the Scampi Bar.

Mrs. Jones was still having hysterics, but Arabel said, "Two masked gunmen stole a diamond brooch and gave it to a squirrel to carry away and he's flown off on Mortimer, who's our raven. Please get him back!"

"Where did the two men go?"

"They just walked off up the High Street."

"All sounds like a fishy tale to me," said the police sergeant—it was the same one who had been in earlier. "You sure you didn't just give the brooch to the bird and tell him to flit off with it to the nearest fence?"

"Oh, how could you say such a thing," wept Mrs. Jones, "when our Mortimer's the best-hearted raven in Rumbury Town, even if he does look a bit sour at times?"

"Any clues?" said the sergeant to his men.

"There's a trail of cheese crumbs here," said a constable. "We'll see how far we can follow them."

The police left, following the trail of cheese,

which led all the way up Rumbury High Street, past the bank, past the fishmonger, past the supermarket, past the ironmonger, past the record shop, past the war memorial, and stopped at the tube station.

"He's outdone us," said the sergeant. "Went on by train. Did a large black bird buy a ticket to anywhere about ten minutes ago?" he asked Mr. Gumbrell, the ticket clerk.

"No."

"He could have got a ticket from a machine," one of the constables pointed out.

"They all say OUT OF ORDER."

"Anyway, why should a bird buy a ticket? He could just fly into a train," said another constable.

All the passengers who had traveled on the Rumberloo line that morning were asked if they had seen a large black bird or a squirrel carrying a diamond brooch. None of them had.

"Please, no offense, Mrs. Jones," said Peter Stone, "but in these doubtful circumstances I'd just as soon you didn't come back after lunch. We'll say nothing about the forty thousand pounds for the brooch at present. Let's hope the bird is caught with it on him."

"He didn't take it," said Arabel. "You'll find out."

Arabel and Mrs. Jones walked home to Number Six, Rainwater Crescent. Arabel was pale and silent, but Mrs. Jones scolded all the way.

"Any bird with a scrap of gumption would have taken the brooch off that wretched little rat of a squirrel. Ashamed of himself, he ought to be! Nothing but trouble and aggravation we've had since Mortimer has been in the family; let's hope that's the last of him."

Arabel said she didn't want any tea, and went to bed, and cried herself to sleep.

When he finished work that evening Mr. Jones went up to the police station and identified the motorcycle as the one that had passed him the night the bank had been robbed.

"How can you be sure it's the same?" the sergeant said.

"The pink flower sticker on the rear fender."

"Good," said the sergeant. "We found a couple of black feathers stuck to the tank. If you ask *me*, that bird's up to his beak in all this murky business."

"How could he be?" Mr. Jones said. "He was just crossing the road when the motorcycle went by."

"Maybe they slipped him the cash as they passed."

"In that case we'd have seen it, wouldn't we? Do you know who the motorcycle belongs to?"

"It was found abandoned on the Rumberloo line embankment, where it comes out of the tunnel. We've a theory, but I'm not telling *you;* your family's under suspicion. Don't leave the district without informing us."

Mr. Jones said he had no intention of leaving. "We want Mortimer found. My daughter's very upset."

Arabel was more than upset, she was in despair. She wandered about the house all day, looking at the things that reminded her of Mortimer—the fireplace bricks without any mortar, the tattered hearthrug, the plates with beak-sized chips missing, the chewed upholstery, all the articles that turned up under carpets and linoleum, and the missing stairs. The carpenter hadn't come yet to replace them, and Mr. Jones was too dejected to nag him.

"I wouldn't have thought I'd get fond of a bird so quick," he said. "I miss his sulky face, and his thoughtful ways, and the sound of him crunching about the house. Eat up your tea, Arabel, dearie, there's a good girl. I expect Mortimer will find his way home by and by."

But Arabel couldn't eat. Tears ran down her nose and onto her bread and jam until it was all soggy. That reminded her of the flood that Mortimer had caused by blocking up the bathroom plug, and the tears rolled even faster. "Mortimer doesn't know our address!" she said. "He doesn't even know our name!"

"We'll offer five pounds' reward for his return," Mr. Jones said.

"Five pounds!" cried Mrs. Jones, who had just come home from the supermarket where she now

worked. "Five pounds you offer for the return of that fiend when already we owe eight hundred and seventeen pounds, seventy-two pence to Round & Round, let alone the forty thousand to Peter Stone? The only thing that makes me thankful is that bird doesn't have to come with me to the supermarket!"

Just the same Mr. Jones stuck up his REWARD sign in the sub post office, alongside one from Peter Stone offering one thousand pounds for information that might lead to the return of his brooch, and similar ones from the bank, ironmonger, and fishmonger.

Meanwhile, what of Mortimer and the squirrel?

They had flown as far as the tube station. There, Sam, by kicking Mortimer in the ribs and punching the top of his head, had directed him to fly into the station entrance.

Rumbury Tube Station is very old. The two entrances have big round arches with sliding openwork iron gates, and the station is faced all over with shiny raw-meat colored tiles. A dark-blue enamel sign says LONDON GENERAL OMNIBUS & SUBTERRANEAN RAILWAY COMPANY. BY APPMNT TO HIS MAJESTY KING EDWARD VII.

For nearly fifty years there had been only one slow, creaking old lift to take people down to the trains. A sign on it said NOT AUTHORIZED TO CARRY MORE THAN 12 PASSENGERS. People too impatient to wait for it had to walk down about a thousand spiral stairs. But lately the station had been modernized by the addition of a handsome pair of escalators, one up, one down, which replaced the spiral stairs. Nothing else was modern: the ticket machines were so old that people said they would work only for a Queen Victoria bun penny, the bookstall was always shut, and had copies of the *Morning Post* for August 4, 1914, covered in dust; the candy machines had been empty for generations, and down below, as well as the train platforms, there were all kinds of mysterious old galleries, for in the days when trams still ran in London it had also been an underground tramway station, connecting with the Kingsway, Aldwych, and Spurgeon's Tabernacle line.

Not many trains stop at Rumbury Station; most of them rush straight through from Nutmeg Hill to Canon's Green.

Old Mr. Gumbrell, the ticket clerk, was Mr. Jones's uncle. Besides selling tickets he also ran the lift. He was too shortsighted to see across to the lift from the ticket office, so he used to count tickets; when he had sold twelve he would lock up his office and take the lift down. This meant that sometimes people had to wait a very long time but it didn't much matter, as there probably wouldn't be a train for hours anyway. However, in the end there were complaints, which was why the escalators were installed. Mr. Gumbrell enjoyed riding on these, which he called escatailors; he used to leave the lift at the bottom and travel back up the moving stairs.

He did this today. He ran the lift slowly down (never noticing that Mortimer, with Sam the squirrel still grimly clutching him, was perched high up near the ceiling on the frame of a poster advertising the Pickwick, the Owl, and the Waverly Pen). Mr. Gumbrell left the lift at the bottom, and sailed back up the escalator, mumbling to himself,

"Arr, these 'ere moving stairs do be an amazing wonder of science. Whatever will they think of next?"

When Mr. Gumbrell got to the top again he found the police there, examining the trail of cheese crumbs which stopped outside the station entrance. They stayed a long time, but Mr. Gumbrell could give them no useful information.

"Birds and squirrels!" he muttered when they had gone. "Is it likely you'd be a-seeing birds and squirrels with di'mond brooches in a tube station?"

The phone rang. There was only one telephone in the station, a public phone booth with the door missing, so if people wanted to call Mr. Gumbrell— which did not often happen—they rang on that line.

This time it was Mr. Jones.

"Is that you, Uncle Arthur?"

"O' course it's me. Who else would it be?"

"We just wondered if you'd seen Arabel's raven. The trail of cheese crumbs led up your way, the police said."

"No, I have not seen a raven," snapped Mr. Gumbrell. "Coppers a-bothering here all afternoon, but still I haven't! Nor I haven't seen a Socrates bird nor a cassodactyl nor a pterowary. This is a tube station, not a zoological garden."

"Will you keep a lookout, just the same?" said Mr. Jones.

Mr. Gumbrell thumped back the receiver. He was fed up with all the bother.

"Do I wait here any longer," he said to himself, "likely the militia and the beef-guards and the horse-eaters and the traffic wardens'll be along, too. I'm closing up."

Rumbury Tube Station was not supposed to be closed except between 1 A.M. and 5 A.M., but in fact old Mr. Gumbrell often did close it earlier if his bad toe was bothering him. No one had complained yet.

"Even if me toe ain't aching now, likely it'll start any minute, with all this willocking about," Mr. Gumbrell argued to himself, and so he switched off the escalators, locked the lift gates and ticket office, turned off the lights, called up Nutmeg Hill and Canon's Green to tell them not to let any trains stop, padlocked the big main mesh gates, and stomped off home to supper.

Next morning there were several people waiting to catch the first train to work when Mr. Gumbrell arrived to open up. They bustled in as soon as he slid the gates back and didn't stop at the ticket office for they all had season tickets. But when they reached the top of the escalator they did stop, in dismay and astonishment.

For the escalators were not there: nothing but a big gaping black hole.

"Someone's pinched the stairs," said a Covent Garden porter.

"Don't be so soft. How could you pinch an escalator?" said a milkman.

"Well, they're gone, aren't they?" said a bus driver. "What's *your* theory? Earthquake? Sunk into the ground?"

"Squatters," said a train driver. "Mark my words, squatters have taken 'em."

"How'd they get through the locked gates? Anyway, what'd they take them *for*?"

"To squat on, of course."

Mr. Gumbrell stood scratching his head. "Took my escatailors," he said sorrowfully. "What did they want to go and do that for? If they'd 'a took the lift, now, I wouldn't 'a minded near as much. Well, all you lot'll have to go down in the lift, anyways—there ain't twelve of ye, so it's all right."

It wasn't all right, though. When he pulled the lever that should have brought the lift to the surface, nothing happened.

"And I'll tell you why," said the train driver, peering through the closed top gates. "Someone's chawed through the lift cable."

"Sawed through it?"

"No, kind of chewed or haggled through; a right messy job. Lucky the current was switched off, or whoever done it would have been frizzled like popcorn."

"Someone's been sabotaging the station," said the bus driver. "Football fans, is my guess."

"Hippies, more like."

"Someone ought to tell the cops."

"Cops!" grumbled Mr. Gumbrell. "Not likely! Had enough of them in yesterday a-scavenging about for ravens and squirrels."

Another reason why he did not want to tell the police was because he was shy about mentioning that he had left the station unattended for so long. But the early travelers, finding they could not get a train there, walked off to the next stop down the line, Nutmeg Hill. They told their friends at work what had happened, and the story spread about. Presently a reporter from the *Rumbury Borough News* rang up the tube station for confirmation of the tale.

"Is that Rumbury Tube Station? Can you tell me, please, if the trains are running normally?"

"Nevermore!" croaked a harsh voice, and the receiver was thumped down.

"You'd better go up there and have a look around," said the *Borough News* editor, when his reporter told him of this puzzling conversation.

So the reporter—his name was Dick Otter—took a bus up to the tube station.

It was a dark, drizzly, foggy day, and when he peered in through the station entrance he thought that it looked like a cave inside, under the round arches— the ticket machines, with their dim little lights, were like stalagmites, the white tiled floor was like a sheet of ice, the empty green candy machines were like hanks of moss dangling against the walls, and old Mr. Gumbrell, with his white whiskers, seated inside the ticket booth, was like some wizened goblin with his little piles of magic cards telling people where they could go.

"Is the station open?" Dick asked.

"*You* walked in, didn't you? But you can't *go* anywhere," said Mr. Gumbrell.

Dick went over and looked at the gaping hole where the escalators used to be. Mr. Gumbrell had hung a couple of chains across, to stop people from falling down.

Then Dick peered through the lift gates and down the shaft.

Then he went back to Mr. Gumbrell, who was reading yesterday's football results by the light of a candle. It was very dark in the station entrance because nearly all the light switches were down below and Mr. Gumbrell could not get at them.

"Who do you think took the escalators?" Dick asked, getting out his notebook.

Mr. Gumbrell had been thinking about this a good deal, on and off, during the morning.

"Spooks," he replied. "Spooks what doesn't like modern inventions. I reckon the station's haunted. As I've bin sitting here this morning, there's a ghostly voice what sometimes comes and croaks in me lughole. 'Nevermore,' it says, 'nevermore.' That's one

reason why I haven't informed the cops. What could
they do? What that voice means is that this station
shall nevermore be used."

"I see," said Dick thoughtfully. In his notebook
he wrote "Is Tube Station Haunted or Is Ticket Clerk
Round the Bend?"

"What else makes you think it's haunted?" he
asked.

"Well," said Mr. Gumbrell, "there couldn't *be* anybody downstairs, could there? I locked up last night, when the nine o'clock south had gone, and I phoned 'em at Nutmeg Hill and Canon's Green not to let any trains stop here till I give 'em the word again. No one would 'a gone down this end after that, and yet sometimes I thinks as I can hear voices down the lift shaft a-calling out 'Help, help.' Which is a contradication of nature, since, like I said, no one could be down there."

"Supposing they'd gone down last night before you locked up?"

"Then they'd 'a caught the nine o'clock south, wouldn't they? No, 'tis ghosties down there all right."

"Whose ghosts, do you think?"

"'Tis the ghosties of they old tramcar drivers. Why do I think that? Well, you look at these 'ere tickets."

Mr. Gumbrell showed a pile of green fifteen-penny tube tickets. Each had a large triangular snip taken from one side.

"See! A ghostie did that!" he said triumphantly. "Who else could 'a got into my ticket office? The only way in was through the slot, see, where the passengers pays their fares. A yuman couldn't get through there, but a ghostie could. It was the ghostie of one of they old tramcar conductors, a-hankering to clip a ticket again like in bygone days, see? And the same ghostie pinched the ham sandwich I'd been a-saving for me breakfast and left nowt but crumbs. That's why I haven't rung Head Office, neether, 'cos what would be the use? If they did put in a pair of new escatailors and fix the lift, the new ones'd be gone again by next day. That's what the voice means when it says, 'Nevermore.'"

"You think you can hear voices crying 'Help, help' down the lift shaft?"

Dick went and listened but there was nothing to be heard at that moment.

"Likely I'm the only man as can hear 'em," said Mr. Gumbrell.

"It seems to me I can smell something though," Dick said, sniffing.

Up from the lift shaft floated the usual smell of tube station—a queer, warm, dusty, metallic smell like powdered ginger. But as well as that there was another smell—fragrant and tantalizing.

"Smells to me like coffee," Dick said.

"There you are, then!" cried Mr. Gumbrell triumphantly. "They old tramcar drivers used to brew up a big pot o' coffee when they was waiting for the last tram back to Brixton of a nighttime."

"I'd like to get some pictures of the station," said Dick, and he went over to the public phone booth and dialed his office, to get a photographer. But as he waited with tenpence in his hand, something large and black suddenly wafted past his head in the gloom, snatched the receiver from him, and whispered harshly in his ear, "Nevermore!"

Next day the *Rumbury Borough News* had headlines:

"IS OUR TUBE STATION HAUNTED? Mr. Gumbrell, ticket collector and clerk there for the last forty years, asserts that it is. 'Ghosts of old-time tramcar drivers sit downstairs,' he says, 'playing dominoes and drinking licorice water.'" (Dick Otter had phoned his story from the phone booth in the sub post office and the girl in the newsroom had misheard "drinking coffee" as "drinking toffee," which she rightly thought was nonsense, so she changed it to "drinking licorice water.")

"Shan't be able to meet people's eyes in the street," said Mrs. Jones at breakfast. "Going balmy, your uncle Arthur is, without a doubt. Haunted police station? Take him along to see the doctor, shall I?"

The postman rang, with a special delivery from a firm of lawyers: Messrs. Gumme, Harbottle, Inkpen, and Rule.

"Dear Madam," it said, "acting as solicitors for Mr. Round and Mr. Toby Round, we wish to know when it will be convenient for you to pay the eight hundred and seventeen pounds, seventy-two pence' worth of damages that you owe our clients for De-struction of Premises?"

This threw Mrs. Jones into a dreadful flutter.

"That I should live to see the day when we are turned out of house and home on account of a bad-tempered fiend of a bird fetched in off the street by my own husband and dragged about in a red wagon by my own daughter!"

"Well, you haven't lived to see the day yet," said Mr. Jones. "Wild creatures, ravens are counted as, in law, so we can't be held responsible for the bird's actions. I'll go around and tell them so, and *you*'d better do something to cheer up Arabel. I've never seen the child so thin and mopey."

He drove his taxi up to Round & Round, the record shop, but, strangely enough, neither Mr. Round nor Mr. Toby Round was to be seen; the place was locked, silent, and dusty.

After trying to persuade Arabel to eat her break-fast—which was no use, as Arabel wouldn't touch it—Mrs. Jones decided to call Uncle Arthur and tell him he should see a doctor for his nerves. She called up the tube station, but the telephone rang and rang and nobody answered. (In fact, the reason for this was that a great many sightseers, having read the piece in the *Borough News*, had come to stare at the station, and Mr. Gumbrell was having a fine time telling them all about the ways of the old tramcar drivers.) While Mrs. Jones was still holding the telephone and listening to the bell ring, another bell rang, louder: the front door bell.

"Trouble, trouble, nothing but trouble," grumbled Mrs. Jones. "Here, Arabel, lovey, hold the phone and say, 'Hallo, Uncle Arthur, Mum wants to speak to you,' if he answers, will you, while I see who's at the front door."

Arabel took the receiver and Mrs. Jones went to the front door where there were two policemen. She let out a screech.

"It's no use that pair of sharks sending you to arrest me for their eight hundred and seventeen pounds—I haven't got it if you were to turn me upside down and shake me till September!"

The police looked puzzled and one of them said, "I reckon there's some mistake. We don't want to turn you upside down—we came to ask if you recognize this?"

He held out a small object in the palm of his hand.

Mrs. Jones had a close look at it.

"Why certainly I do," she said. "That's Mr. Round's tiepin—the one he had made out of one of his back teeth when it fell out as he ate a plateful of Irish stew."

Meanwhile, Arabel was still sitting on the stairs holding the phone to her ear, when all at once she heard a hoarse whisper:

"Nevermore!"

Arabel was so astonished she almost dropped the telephone. She looked all around her—nobody there. Then she looked back at the phone, but it had gone silent again. After a minute a different voice barked, "Who's that?"

"Hullo, Uncle Arthur, it's me, Arabel. Mum wants to speak to you."

"Well, I don't want to speak to her," said Mr. Gumbrell, and he hung up.

Arabel sat on the stairs and she said to herself,

"That was Mortimer and he must be up at the tube station because that's where Uncle Arthur is."

Arabel had often traveled by tube and knew the way to the station. She got her red wagon, and she put on her thick warm woolly coat, and she went out the back door because her mother was still talking at the front and Arabel didn't want to be stopped. She walked up the High Street, past the bank. The manager looked out and said to himself, "That child's too young to be out on her own. I'd better follow her and find who she belongs to."

He started after her.

Next Arabel passed the supermarket. The manager looked out and said to himself, "That's Mrs. Jones's little girl. I'll just nip after her and ask her where her mother's got to today." So he followed Arabel.

Then she passed the Round & Round record shop, but there was nobody in it, and Mr. Jones had become tired of waiting and driven off in his taxi.

Then she passed Peter Stone, the jeweler's. Peter Stone saw her through the window and thought, "That girl looks as if she knows where she means to go. And she was the only one who showed any sense after my burglary. Maybe it was a true story about the squirrel and the raven. Anyway, no harm following her, to see where she goes." So he locked up his shop and followed.

Arabel passed the fire station. Usually the fire-men waved to her—they had been friendly ever since they'd had to come and climb in the Joneses' bathroom window—but today they were all hastily pulling on their helmets and rushing about. And just as she had passed on, the fire engine shot out into the street going lickety-split.

Presently Arabel came to the tube station. The first person she saw there was her great-aunt Annie Gumbrell.

"*Arabel Jones!* What are you doing walking up the High Street by yourself, liable to get run over and kidnapped and murdered and abducted and worse? The idea! Where's your mother? And where are you going?"

"I'm looking for Mortimer," said Arabel, and she kept on going. "I've stayed on the same side all the way; I didn't have to cross over," she said over her shoulder as she went into the tube station.

Aunt Annie had come up to the station to tell Uncle Arthur that he was behaving foolishly and had better come home, but she couldn't get near him be-cause of the crowd. In fact, Arabel was the only per-son who *could* get into the station entrance now, because she was so small—there was just room for her and then the place was completely crammed. Aunt Annie wasn't able to get in at all. When Arabel was inside somebody kindly picked her up and set her on top of the fivepenny ticket machine so that she could see.

"What's happening?" she asked.

"They reckon someone's stuck in the lift, down at the bottom. So they're a-going to send down a fireman, and he'll go in through the trapdoor in the roof of the lift and fetch 'em back," said her great-uncle Arthur, who happened to be standing by her. "I've told 'em and told 'em 'tis the ghosties of old tram drivers, but they don't take no notice."

"Why don't they just have a train from Nutmeg Hill stop down below and someone from it go to see what the matter is?"

"Train drivers' union won't let 'em stop. They say if 'tis the ghosties of old tram drivers stuck in the lift, 'tis a different union and no concern of theirn."

Now the firemen, who had been taking a careful look at the lift, asked everybody to please step out into the street to make room. Then they rigged up a light, because the station was so dark, and they brought in a little minihelicopter, which was mostly used for rescuing people who got stuck on church spires or the roofs of burning buildings, but they had worked out that it would be just the right size to go down the lift shaft if the pilot steered with care. So down it went, and the whole population of Rumbury Town, by now standing in the street outside, said, "Coo!" and held their breath.

Presently a shout came from below.

"They've found someone," said the firemen, and everybody said, "Coo!" again and held their breath some more.

Just at this moment Arabel (still sitting on the fivepenny ticket machine for she was in no one's way there) felt a thump on her right shoulder. It was lucky that she had put on her thick warm woolly coat, for two claws took hold of her shoulder with a grip like a bulldog clip, and a loving croak in her ear said, *"Nevermore!"*

"Mortimer!" cried Arabel, and she was so pleased that she might have toppled off the ticket machine if

Mortimer hadn't spread out his wings like a tightrope walker's umbrella and balanced them both.

Mortimer was just as pleased to see Arabel as she was to see him. When he had them both balanced he wrapped his left-hand wing around her and said, "Nevermore" five or six times over, in tones of great satisfaction and enthusiasm.

"Look, Mortimer, they're bringing someone up."

The minihelicopter had room for only one passenger at a time. Up it crept, buzzing like a mosquito, dangled by the lift shaft, and who should climb out but Mr. Toby Round, looking hungry and sorry for himself. The minute he had landed all sorts of helpful people, St. John ambulance men and stretcher bearers and clergymen and the matron of the Rumbury Hospital, all rushed at him with bandages and cups of tea and said, "Are you all right?"

They would have taken him away, but he said he wanted to wait for his brother.

The minicopter had gone down again at once. In a minute up it came with the other Mr. Round. As soon as he landed he noticed Arabel and Mortimer, perched on the ticket machine, and the sight of them seemed to set him in a passion.

"Grab that bird!" he shouted. "*He's* the cause of all the trouble! Gnawed through the lift cable and ate the escalator and had my brother and me trapped in utter discomfort for forty-eight hours!"

"And what was you a-doing down there," said Mr. Gumbrell suspiciously, "after the nine o'clock south had come and gone?"

Just at this moment a whole truckload of police arrived with Mrs. Jones, who seemed half distracted.

"*There* you are!" she screamed when she saw Arabel. "And me nearly frantic. *Oh* my goodness, there's that great awful bird, as if we hadn't enough to worry us!"

But the police swarmed about the Round brothers, and the sergeant said, "I have a warrant to arrest you two on suspicion of having pinched the cash from the bank last month and if you want to know why we think it's you that did it, it's because we found your tooth tiepin left behind in the safe and one of Toby's fingerprints on the abandoned motorcycle, and I shouldn't wonder if you did the jobs at the supermarket and the jeweler's and all the others, too."

"It's not true!" shouted Mr. Toby Round. "We didn't do it! We didn't do *any* of them. We were staying with my sister-in-law at Romford on each occasion. Her name's Mrs. Flossie Wilkes and she lives at 2001 Station Approach. If you ask *my* opinion that raven is the thief—"

But the sergeant had pulled Mr. Toby Round's hand from his pocket to put a handcuff on it, and when he did so, what should come out as well but Sam the squirrel, and what should Sam be clutching in his paws but Mr. Peter Stone's diamond brooch worth forty thousand pounds.

So everybody said, "Coo," again.

And Mr. Round and Mr. Toby Round were taken off to Rumbury Hill Police Station.

The police sergeant hitched a ride in the firemen's minicopter and went down the lift shaft and had a look around the old galleries and disused tram station, and he found the money that had been stolen from the bank, all packed in the plastic garbage cans that had been stolen from Brown's the ironmongers and he found nine hundred and ninety-nine of the two thousand cans of best Jamaica blend coffee stolen from the supermarket, and a whole lot of other things that had been stolen from different premises all over Rumbury Town.

While he was making these exciting discoveries down below, up above, Mrs. Jones was saying, "Arabel, you come home directly, and don't you dare go out on your own ever again!"

"Nevermore!" said Mortimer.

So Arabel climbed down, with Mortimer still on her shoulder.

"Here!" said Uncle Arthur, who had been silent for a long time, turning things over in his mind, "that bird ought to be arrested, too, if he's the one what ate my escatailors and put my lift out of order, and how do we know he didn't help those blokes with their burglaries? He was the one what helped the squirrel make off with the di'mond brooch."

"He was flyjacked; he couldn't help it," said Arabel.

"Far from being arrested," said the bank manager, "he'll get a reward from the bank for helping to bring the criminals to justice."

"And he'll get one from me, too," said Peter Stone.

"And from me," said the supermarket manager.

"Come along, Arabel, do," said Mrs. Jones. "Oh my gracious, look at the time, your father'll be home wanting his tea and wondering where in the world we've got to."

Arabel collected her red wagon, which she had left outside, and Mortimer climbed onto it.

"My stars!" cried Mrs. Jones. "You're not going to pull that great black sulky bird all the way home in the wagon when we know perfectly *well* he can fly, the lazy thing, never did I hear anything so outrageous, never!"

"He likes being pulled," said Arabel, so that was the way they went home. The bank manager and the supermarket manager and Mr. Peter Stone and quite a lot of other people saw them as far as the gate.

Mr. Jones was inside and had just made a pot of tea. When he saw them come in the front gate he poured out an eggcupful for Mortimer.

The Bread Bin

All this happened one terrible wild, wet week in February when Mortimer the raven had been living with Arabel Jones in Rumbury Town for several months.

The weather had been so dreadful for so long that everybody in the Jones family was, if not in a bad temper, at least less cheerful than usual. Mrs. Jones complained that even the bread felt damp unless it was made into toast. Arabel had a sniffle, Mr. Jones found it very tiring having to drive his taxi through pouring rain along greasy, skiddy streets day after day, and Mortimer the raven was annoyed because there were two things he wanted to do, and he was not permitted to do either of them. He wanted to be given a ride round the garden in Arabel's red wagon; Mrs. Jones would not allow it because of the weather; and he wanted to climb into the bread bin and go to sleep there. It seemed to him very unreasonable that he wasn't allowed to do this.

"We could keep the bread somewhere else," Arabel said.

"So I buy a bread bin that costs me ninety-five new pence for a great, fat, sulky, lazy bird to sleep in? What's wrong with the coal scuttle? He's slept in *that* for the last three weeks. It's suddenly not comfortable anymore?"

Mrs. Jones had just come back from shopping, very wet. She began taking groceries from her tartan wheeled shopping bag and dumping them on the floor.

"He wants a change," said Arabel, looking out of the window at the gray lines of rain that went slamming across the garden like telegraph wires.

"Naturally! Ginger marmalade on muffins that bird gets for his breakfast, spaghetti and meatballs for lunch, brandy snaps for supper, allowed to sit inside the grandfather clock and slide down the stairs on my best tray with the painted gladioli whenever he wants to, and he must have a *change*, as well? That bird gets more attention than the lord mayor of Hyderabad."

"He doesn't know that," said Arabel. "He hasn't been to Hyderabad."

Arabel and Mortimer went into the front hall. Arabel balanced Mortimer on one of her roller skates and tied a bit of string to it and pulled him around the downstairs part of the house. But neither of them cheered up much. Arabel's throat felt tickly and Mortimer rode along with his head sunk down between his shoulders and his beak sunk down among his feathers, and his feathers all higgledy-piggledy, as if he didn't care which way they pointed.

The telephone rang.

Mortimer would have liked to answer it—he loved answering the telephone—but he had one of his toenails caught in the roller skate; kicking and flapping to free himself he started the skate rolling, shot across the kitchen, knocked over Mrs. Jones's vegetable rack (which had a box of brussels sprouts balanced on top of it), and cannoned against a bag of coffee beans and a container of oven spray, which began shooting out a thick frothy foam. A fierce white smoke came off the foam which made everyone cough. Mrs. Jones rushed to open the window. A lot of wind and rain blew in. A jar of daffodils on the windowsill fell over, and Mortimer quickly pushed some daffodils under the kitchen mat; sliding things underneath mats or linoleum was one of his favorite hobbies.

Arabel mopped up the water that had spilled from the jar. Mrs. Jones wiped up the oven spray foam with a lot of paper towels. The phone went on ringing.

Mortimer suddenly noticed the open window; he climbed up the handles of the drawers under the kitchen sink, very fast, claw over claw, scrabbled his way along the side of the sink, up onto the windowsill, and looked out into the wild, wet, windy garden.

"Drat that phone!" said Mrs. Jones, and rushed to answer it. "Don't touch the foam." But just as she got there the phone stopped ringing.

Mortimer noticed that Arabel's red wagon was just outside the window, down below on the grass, with half an inch of rain in it.

"Mortimer!" said Arabel. "Come back! You'll get wet."

Mortimer took no notice. There were half a dozen horse chestnuts floating in the red wagon. The next-door cat, Ginger, was sitting under a wheelbarrow, trying to keep dry. Mortimer jumped out into the wagon (he was up to his black, feathery knees in water) and began throwing chestnuts at Ginger. He was a very good shot.

"Mortimer!" said Arabel, hanging out of the window. "You are not to throw conkers at Ginger. He's never done you any harm."

Mortimer took no notice. He threw another conker.

Arabel wriggled back off the draining board, opened the back door, ran out into the garden, grabbed the handle of the wagon, and pulled it back indoors with Mortimer on board.

Some of the water slopped onto the kitchen floor.

"*Arabel!*" said Mrs. Jones, coming back into the kitchen. "Have you been out of doors in your bedroom slippers? Oh my stars, if you don't catch your mortal end my name's Mrs. Gipsy Petulengro. And where's all this water come from?"

"I only went to fetch Mortimer, because he was getting wet," Arabel said. "I stayed on the path."

"Getting wet?" said Mrs. Jones. "Why shouldn't he get wet? Birds are *meant* to get wet. So you think we should dry him off with the hair dryer?"

She shoved the wagon outside and slammed the door.

The phone began to ring once more.

Arabel thought the hair dryer was a good idea. While Mrs. Jones hurried back to the telephone, Arabel got the dryer out of its box, plugged it in, and

started blowing Mortimer dry. All his feathers stood straight up, making him look like a turkey. He was so astonished that he shouted, "Nevermore!" and stepped backward into a pan of bread rolls that were waiting to go into the oven. He sank into them up to his ankles and left bird's-claw footprints all along them. But he enjoyed being dried and turned around and around so that Arabel could blow him all over, in between every feather.

"That was Auntie Brenda," said Mrs. Jones, coming back. "She says she's taking her lot roller-skating at the rink, and she'll stop by and pick us up, too."

"Oh," said Arabel.

"Don't you *want* to go roller-skating?" said Mrs. Jones.

"Well, I expect Mortimer will enjoy it," said Arabel.

"I just hope he doesn't disgrace us," said Mrs. Jones, giving Mortimer a dark look. "But I'm not going out and leaving him alone in the house. Never shall I forget, not if I should live to eighty and be elected beauty queen of Lancaster, the time we went to the movies and when we got back he'd eaten the banisters and the bathroom basin complete, and two and a half packets of assorted rainbow Bath Oil Bubble Gums."

"Nevermore," said Mortimer.

"Promises, promises," said Mrs. Jones.

"The house looked lovely, all full of bubbles," Arabel said. "Mortimer thought so, too."

"Anyway, he's not having the chance to do it again. Put your coat on; Auntie Brenda will be here in ten minutes."

Arabel put her coat on slowly. Her throat tickled more and more; she did not feel like going out in the wet and cold. Also, although they were her cousins, she was not very fond of Aunt Brenda's lot. There were three of them: their names were Lindy, Cindy, and Mindy. As a matter of fact, they were horrible girls. They had unkind natures and liked saying things that hurt other people's feelings. They were always eating, not because they were hungry, but just because they were greedy: Life Savers and bags of chips and bottles of Coke. They had more toys than they could be bothered to play with. And they had a lot of spots, too.

They had not yet met Mortimer.

Aunt Brenda stopped outside the house in her shiny car.

Cindy, Lindy, and Mindy put their heads out of the window and stopped eating chocolate macaroni sticks long enough to scream,

"Hallo, Arabel! We've got new coats, new boots, new furry hoods, new furry gloves, new skirts, and new roller skates!"

"Spoiled lot," muttered Mrs. Jones, putting Arabel's old skates in her tartan shopping bag on wheels. "So what was wrong with the old ones, I should like to know? Anyone would think their dad was the president of the Bank of Monte Carlo."

In fact, their dad was a salesman in do-it-yourself wardrobe kits; he traveled so much that he was hardly ever at home.

Arabel went out to the car in her old coat, old hood, old gloves, and old boots. She held Mortimer tightly. He was very interested at sight of the car; his black eyes shone like black satin buttons.

"We're going in that car, Mortimer," Arabel said to him.

"Kaaaark," said Mortimer.

Lindy and Cindy hung out of the back window shouting, "Arabel, Arabel, 'orrible Arabel, 'orrible, 'orrible, 'orrible Arabel." Then they spotted Mortimer and their eyes went as round as LP records.

"Coo!" said Cindy. "What's *that*?"

"What *have* you got there, 'orrible Arabel?" said Lindy.

"He's my raven, Mortimer," said Arabel.

All three girls burst into screams of laughter.

"A raven? What d'you want a *raven* for? He's not a raven anyway—he's just an old molting jackdaw. What's the use of him? Can he speak?"

"If he wants to," said Arabel.

Cindy, Lindy, and Mindy laughed even louder.

"I bet all he can say is caw! See, saw, old Jacky Daw. All he can say is croak and caw!"

"Stop teasing, girls, and make room for Arabel in the back," said Auntie Brenda.

Arabel and Mortimer got into the back and sat quietly. Cindy tried to give Mortimer's tail feathers a tweak, but he flashed her such a threatening look from his black eyes that she changed her mind.

Mrs. Jones got into the front beside her sister Brenda, and they were off.

Mortimer liked riding in a car. As soon as he was fairly sure that Arabel's cousins were not going to attack him at once, he began to bounce up and down gently on Arabel's shoulder, looking out at the shops of Rumbury High Street flashing past, at the red buses swishing along, at the streetlamps like a necklace of salmon-colored flowers, and the greengrocers all red and orange and yellow and green.

"Nevermore," he muttered. "Nevermore."

"There, you see," said Arabel. "He *can* speak."

"But what does he mean?" tittered Mindy.

"He means that where he comes from they don't have buses and greengrocers and streetlamps."

"Oh, what rubbish! I don't believe you know what he means at all."

Arabel kept silent after that.

When they reached Rumbury Borough Roller Skating Rink Mortimer was even more amazed at the big sign, all picked out in pink lights, and the entrance, paved with yellow glass tiles.

"You get the tickets, Martha, I'll put the car in the car park," said Auntie Brenda.

Arabel's three cousins were all expert roller skaters. They came to the rink two or three times a week. They buckled on their new skates and shot off into the middle, knocking over any amount of people on the way.

Arabel, when she had put on her skates, went slowly and carefully around the edge. She did not want to be bumped because Mortimer was still on her shoulder. Also she felt very tired and her throat had stopped tickling and was now really sore. And her head ached.

Auntie Brenda came back from putting away the car and sat down by Mrs. Jones and the two sisters began talking.

"We'll have to stay here for hours yet," thought Arabel.

"Come on into the middle, cowardy custard! Caw, caw, cowardy, cowardy!" screamed Lindy and Cindy.

"Yes, go on, ducky, you'll be all right, don't be afraid," called Auntie Brenda. But Arabel shook her head and stuck to the edge.

Mortimer was having a lovely time. He didn't mind Arabel going so slowly because he was looking around at all the other skaters. He admired the way they whizzed in and out and round and through and past and in and out and round. He dug his claws lovingly into Arabel's shoulder.

"I wish I had three roller skates, Mortimer," Arabel said. "Then you could ride on the third one."

Mortimer wished it, too.

"Tell you what," Arabel said. "I'll take my skates off. I don't feel much like skating."

She sat down at the edge, took her skates off, carried one, and lifted Mortimer onto the other, which she pulled along by the laces.

"Cooo!" shrieked Cindy, whirling past. "Look at scaredy-baby Arabel, pulling her silly old rook along."

"Around the rolling rink the ragged rookie rumbles," screeched Mindy.

"Scared to skate, scared to skate," chanted Lindy.

They really were horrible girls.

Arabel went very slowly over to where her mother and Auntie Brenda were sitting.

"Can I go home, please, Ma?" she said. "My legs ache."

"Oh, go on, ducky, have another try," said Auntie Brenda cheerfully. "There's nothing to be scared of, really there isn't."

But Mrs. Jones looked carefully at her daughter and said, "Don't you feel well, lovey?"

"No," said Arabel, and two tears rolled slowly down her cheeks. Mrs. Jones put a hand on Arabel's forehead.

"It's quite hot," she said. "I think we'd better go home, Brenda."

"Can't she stay another half hour?"

Mrs. Jones shook her head. "I don't think she should."

"Oh my goodness," said Auntie Brenda rather

crossly. "The girls *will* be disappointed." But she raised her voice in a terrific shout. "Cindy! Lindy! Miiiiindy! Come along—your cousin's not feeling well."

Arabel's three cousins came trailing slowly across the rink with sulky expressions.

"*Now* what?" said Mindy.

"We only just got here," said Cindy.

"Just because 'orrible Arabel can't skate—," said Lindy.

"Can't Ma and I go home by bus?" said Arabel.

Auntie Brenda and the three girls looked hopeful, but Mrs. Jones said, "I really think we ought to get home as quickly as we can. Besides, I've left my shopping bag in the trunk of your car, Brenda."

"Oh, very well," said Brenda crossly. "Come along, girls."

They all trailed off to the parking garage. Aunt Brenda's car was up on the fourth level.

"Not worth waiting for the lift," Brenda said.

They had to climb a lot of steps. Arabel's legs ached worse and worse. But Mortimer was even more interested by the parking garage than he had been by the rink. Arabel was carrying him, with her skates. Mortimer gazed around with astonishment, at the huge concrete slopes, and the huge level stretches, covered with cars. His black eyes sparkled like gumdrops.

Arabel's arms ached almost as much as her legs. While Auntie Brenda was finding her car key at the bottom of her bag and unlocking the car, Arabel put her skates down on the ground.

With a quick wriggle, Mortimer flopped out of Arabel's grasp and climbed onto one of her skates. Then he half spread his wings and gave himself a mighty shove off. The roller skate, with Mortimer sitting on it, went whizzing along the flat concrete runway, between two rows of cars.

"Oh, stop him, stop him!" Arabel said. "He'll go down the ramp!"

She meant to shout, but the words came out in a whisper.

Lindy, Mindy, and Cindy rushed after Mortimer. But they were too late to catch him. He shot down the ramp onto the third level.

"Nevermore, nevermore, *nevermore*," he shouted joyfully, and gave himself another shove with his wings, which sent him up the ramp on the opposite side, and back onto the fourth level.

"There he goes, there!" cried Auntie Brenda. "After him, girls!" But Lindy, Mindy, and Cindy were now out of earshot, down on the third level.

"Oh goodness gracious me, did you ever see anything so provoking in all your born *days*," said Mrs. Jones. "I never did, not even when I worked at the invisible menders'. Don't you go running after that wretched feathered monster, Arabel, you stay right here."

But Arabel had followed Mortimer up onto the fifth level.

"Mortimer! Please come back!" she called in her voice that would not rise any louder than a whisper. "*Please* come back. I don't feel well. I'll bring you here again another day."

Mortimer didn't hear her. Up on the fifth level the wind was icy cold and whistled like a saw blade. Arabel began to shiver and couldn't stop. Mortimer was having a wonderful time, shooting up and down ramps, in and out between cars, rowing himself along

with his wings at a tremendous rate. Other car owners began running after him.

"Stop that bird!" shouted Auntie Brenda. Lots of
people tried. But Mortimer was going so fast that it
was easy for him to dodge them; he had discovered
the knack of steering the roller skate with his tail,
and he spun around corners and in between people's

legs as if he were entered for the All-Europe Raven Bobsleigh Finals.

After ten minutes there must have been at least fifty people chasing from one ramp to another, all over the parking garage.

Finally Mortimer was caught quite by chance when a stout lady, who had just come in from an outside entrance, stuck out her umbrella to twirl the rain off it before closing it; Mortimer, swinging around a Ford Capri on one wheel, ran full tilt into the umbrella and got caught among the spokes. By the time he was disentangled, Auntie Brenda, very cross, had come up and seized him by the scruff of his neck.

"Now perhaps we can get going," she snapped, and carried him back to her car. "I'll put him in your shopper, Martha," she said grimly, "then he won't be able to get loose again. I really don't know why you wanted to come roller-skating with a *raven*."

Mrs. Jones was too worried about Arabel to answer.

Presently Lindy, Cindy, and Mindy came panting and straggling back, and Arabel walked slowly up from the third level. She couldn't stop shivering.

"Where's Mortimer?" she whispered.

"He's in the trunk and there he'll stay till you get home," said Auntie Brenda. "That bird's a disgrace."

Arabel started to say, "He didn't know he was doing anything wrong. He thought the parking garage was a skating rink for ravens," but the words stuck inside, as if her throat was full of grit.

By the time they arrived at the Joneses' house, Number Six, Rainwater Crescent, Arabel was crying as well as shivering.

She couldn't seem to stop doing either of those things.

Mrs. Jones jumped out of the car and almost carried Arabel into the house.

"Your shopper!" Auntie Brenda shouted after them, getting the tartan bag out of the trunk.

"Stick it in the front hall, Brenda."

Brenda did. But she and Martha had exactly similar bags on wheels. They had bought them together at a grand clearance sale in Rumbury Bargain Basement Bazaar. Brenda put the wrong bag in the front hall. She left in her trunk the one that still contained Mortimer. As well as Mortimer, it held two pounds of ripe bananas; Mortimer, who loved bananas, was too busy eating them just then to complain about being shut inside the bag.

"We'd better get home quick," Auntie Brenda said. "We won't hang about in case Arabel's got something catching."

She had to make three stops on the way home, however, for Cindy wanted a Dairy Isobar, Lindy wanted a Hokey-Coke, and Mindy wanted a bag of

Chewy Gooeys. All these had to be bought at different shops. By the time they reached their house Mortimer had finished the bananas and was ready to be unzipped from the shopping bag.

When Auntie Brenda undid the zip, expecting to see two boxes of raspberry ice cream, half a dozen electric lightbulbs, and a head of celery, out shot Mortimer, leaving behind him an utter tangle of empty rinds and squashed banana pulp.

"Oh my dear cats alive," said Auntie Brenda. Mortimer was so smothered in banana pulp that for a moment she did not even recognize him. Then she cried, "Girls! It's that bird! Catch the horrible brute. He needs teaching a lesson, that bird does."

Lindy grabbed a walking stick, Cindy got a tennis racket, and Mindy found a shrimping net left over from last summer at Prittlewell on Sea. They started chasing Mortimer about their house. Mortimer never flew if he could help it; he preferred walking at a dignified pace; but just now it seemed best to fly. Getting his wings to open was difficult at first, because of all the mashed banana, but he managed it. He flew to the drawing-room mantelpiece. Mindy took a swipe at him with her shrimping net and knocked off the clock under its glass dome. Mortimer moved himself to the hanging light in the middle of the room and dangled from it upside down, shaking off lumps of

banana. Cindy whirled her racket and knocked the
light through the window. Mortimer flew to the top of
the bookshelf. Lindy tried to hook him with her walking stick and broke the glass front of the bookcase.

"Use your hands, nincompoops," shouted Auntie
Brenda. "You're breaking the place up."

So they dropped their sticks and rackets and nets
and went after Mortimer with their hands. Mortimer
never, never pecked Arabel. But then she never tried
to pull his tail, or grab him by the leg, or snatch hold

of his wing; fairly soon Cindy, Lindy, and Mindy were covered with peck marks and bleeding here and there.

Aunt Brenda tried throwing a tablecloth over Mortimer. That didn't work. She knocked over a table lamp and a jar of chrysanthemums. But after a long chase she managed to get him cornered in the fireplace. The fire was not lighted.

Mortimer went up the chimney.

"Now we've got him," said Auntie Brenda.

"He'll fly out of the top," said Lindy.

"He can't, there's a cowl on it," said Cindy.

They could hear Mortimer, scrabbling in the chimney and muttering, "Nevermore," to himself.

Auntie Brenda telephoned the chimney sweep, whose name was Ephraim Suckett, and asked him to come around at once.

In ten minutes he arrived, with his long flexible rods, and his brushes, and his huge vacuum cleaner.

"Been having a party?" he asked, as he looked around the drawing room. "Wonderful larks these teenagers get up to nowadays."

"We've got a bird in the chimney," Aunt Brenda said grimly. "I want you to get him out."

"A bird, eh?" said Mr. Suckett cautiously, looking at the damage. "He wouldn't be one o' them anacondors with a wingspread of twenty foot? If so I want to make sure I'm covered under my Industrial Injuries Policy."

"He's an ordinary, common raven," snapped Auntie Brenda, "and I'd like you to get him out of that chimney as quickly as you can. I want to light the fire."

So Mr. Suckett poked one of his rods up the chimney as far as it would go, and then screwed another one onto it and poked that up, and then screwed another one onto that. A lot of soot fell into the hearth.

"When did you last have this chimney swept?" Mr. Suckett asked. "Coronation year?"

Mortimer retired farther up the chimney.

Meanwhile, what had happened to Arabel?

She had gone to the hospital.

Mrs. Jones called the doctor as soon as she was indoors. The doctor came quickly and said that Arabel had a bad case of flu and would be better off in Rumbury Central, so Mr. Jones, who had just arrived home for his tea, drove her there at once in the family taxi, wrapped up in three pink blankets, with her feet on a hot-water bottle.

"Where's Mortimer? Is he all right?" Arabel asked faintly in the taxi. "What about his tea?"

"Father'll give him his tea when he gets home," said Mrs. Jones. She had forgotten that, so far as she knew, Mortimer was still in the tartan shopping bag.

Mr. Jones left his wife and daughter at the hospital. Mrs. Jones was going to stay there with Arabel. He drove home. In the front hall he found a tartan shopping bag containing two boxes of raspberry ice cream, some electric lightbulbs, and a head of celery. He put these things away. "Wonder why Martha got all those lightbulbs?" he thought. "She must know there are plenty in the tool cupboard."

He made himself a pot of tea and a large dish of spaghetti, which was the only thing he knew how to cook. Then it struck him that the house was very quiet. Usually when Mortimer was awake there would be a scrunching, or a scraping, or a tapping, or a tinkling, as the raven carefully took something to pieces, or knocked something over, or pushed one thing under another thing.

"Mortimer!" called Mr. Jones. "Where are you? Come out! What are you doing?"

There was no answer. Nobody said, "Nevermore." The house remained quite silent.

Mr. Jones began to feel anxious. In a quiet way, he was fond of Mortimer. Also he wanted to be sure the raven was not eating the back wall of the house, or unraveling the bath towels (Mortimer could take a whole bath towel to pieces in three and a half minutes flat), or munching up the *Home Handyman's Encyclopedia* in ten volumes. Or anything else.

Mr. Jones hunted all over the house for Mortimer and couldn't find him anywhere.

"Oh my goodness," he thought. "The bird must

have wandered out while we were getting Arabel into the taxi. She will be upset. However will we be able to break it to her? She thinks the world of Mortimer."

Just at that moment the telephone rang.

When Mr. Jones picked the phone up, words came out of it in a solid shriek.

"What's that?" said Mr. Jones, listening. "Who is it? This is Jones's Taxi Service here. Is that *you*, Brenda? Is something the matter?"

The shriek went on. All Mr. Jones could distinguish was something about chrysanthemums, and something about soot, and something about a clock.

"Soot in the clock," he thought. "That's unusual. Maybe they've got an oil-fired clock, I daresay such things do exist, and Brenda's always been dead keen on the latest gadgets." "I can't help you, Brenda, I'm afraid," he said into the telephone. "I don't know much about oil-fired clocks, nothing at all, really. You'll have to wait till Arthur gets home. We're all at sixes and sevens here because Arabel's gone to the hospital." And he hung up; he had more things to worry about than soot in his sister-in-law's clock.

Meanwhile, what had been happening to Mortimer?

Mr. Suckett, the sweep, had fastened more and more rods together and poked them farther and farther up Brenda's chimney. Mortimer had retired right up to the very top, but he couldn't get out because of the cowl, though he could look out through the slits. He had a good view and found it very interesting, for Brenda's house was right on top of Rumbury Hill and he could see for miles.

The sweep had got his big vacuum cleaner switched on, and with its nozzle he was sucking up the bales and bales of soot that kept tumbling down the chimney as Mortimer climbed higher and higher.

At last, finding that he could not dislodge Mortimer with his rods, Mr. Suckett began pulling them down again and unscrewing them one by one.

"What'll you do now?" asked Lindy.

"Will you have to take the top of the chimney off?" said Mindy.

"Shall we light a fire and toast him?" said Cindy.

"Just get rid of him *somehow* and be quick about it," said Auntie Brenda.

"We'll have to suck him out," said the sweep.

He withdrew the last of his rods and wheeled the vacuum cleaner close to the fireplace.

This cleaner was like an ordinary household one, but about eight times larger. It had a big canvas drum on wheels, the size of a tar barrel, into which all the soot was sucked. Then, when he had finished a job, the sweep took it away and sold the soot to people at twenty-five pence a pound to put on their slugs. Better than orange peel, he said it was.

By now the canvas drum was packed to bursting with all the soot that had been in Auntie Brenda's chimney, piling up since Coronation year.

Mr. Suckett shoved the nozzle up the chimney and switched on the motor.

It was tremendously powerful. It could suck a Saint Bernard dog right off its feet and up a ten-foot ramp at an angle of thirty degrees. It sucked Mortimer down the chimney like one of his own feathers.

He shot down the chimney, along the canvas tube, and ended up inside the canvas drum, stuffed in with a hundredweight of soot.

Mortimer had quite enjoyed being in the chimney where, if dark, it was interesting; besides, there was the view from the top.

But he did not enjoy being sucked down so fast— upside down as it happened—and even less did he like being packed into a bag full of stifling black powder.

He began to kick and flap and peck and shout, "Nevermore"; in less time than it takes to tell he had torn and clawed a huge hole in the side of the canvas drum; he burst out through this hole like a black bombshell and a hundredweight of soot followed him.

Auntie Brenda had opened all the windows when Mr. Suckett began poking his rods up the chimney, to get rid of the smell of soot. Mortimer went out

through a window with the speed of a Boeing 707; he had had enough of Auntie Brenda's house.

He left a scene of such blackness and muddle behind him that I do not really think it would be worth trying to describe it.

As soon as Mortimer was a short distance away from the house he planed down onto the ground and started to walk home. He really disapproved of flying. He had not the least idea where Auntie Brenda's house was, nor where the Joneses' house was, but he did not worry about that. Since Auntie Brenda's house was on the top of a hill he walked downhill, and he looked at each door as he passed it in hopes it would seem familiar. None did, so he went on, not very fast.

Mr. Jones was at home, unhappily eating spaghetti, and wondering if he should call up the hospital and ask how Arabel was getting on, when the telephone rang.

It was Mrs. Jones.

"Is that you, Ben?" she said. "Oh dear, Ben, poor Arabel's ever so ill, tossing and turning and deliriated, and she keeps asking for Mortimer, and the doctor said you'd better bring him."

Mr. Jones's heart fell into his sheepskin slippers.

"Mortimer's not here," he said.

"Not *there*? Whatever do you mean, Ben, he must be there." Then for the first time Mrs. Jones remembered and let out a guilty gulp. "Oh bless my soul, whatever will I forget next? I quite forgot that poor bird, though goodness knows the bother he caused a couple of hours shut up in a bag will just about serve him right for all his troublesomeness, but you'd better let him out right away, poor thing."

"Let him out of where?"

"My tartan shopping bag. He's inside it."

"No, he's not, Martha," said Mr. Jones. "There was a head of celery, two family-size boxes of raspberry ice cream, and a dozen hundred-watt bulbs.

What did you want to get all those for? We had some already."

Mrs. Jones let out another squawk. "Oh my goodness, then he must be at Brenda's. She must have taken the wrong bag by mistake. You'd better go around there and collect him, Ben, and bring him to the hospital. And when you come, bring two more of Arabel's nighties, and some tea bags, and my digestive mints."

"Around at Brenda's, is he," said Mr. Jones slowly. A lot of things began to make sense: the soot and the clock and the chrysanthemums. "All right, Martha, I'll go and get him and bring him as fast as I can."

He did not tell Martha about the clock and the chrysanthemums. He hung up and then dialed Brenda's number.

There was no reply. In fact, her line seemed to be out of order; he could hear a kind of muffled sound at the other end, but that was all.

It was not hard to guess that if there had been some kind of trouble at Brenda's house, then Mortimer the raven was somehow connected with that trouble.

Mr. Jones scratched his head. Then he took off his slippers and put on his shoes and overcoat. Sighing, he drove his taxi out of its shed and slowly up to where Rainwater Crescent meets Rumbury High

Street. There are four traffic lights at this junction, or should be; this evening they did not seem to be working.

The traffic was in a horrible tangle; two policemen were trying to sort it out, and a third was inspecting, with the help of a torch, the chewed stumps that were all that was left of the traffic lights.

"Evening, Sid," said Mr. Jones, putting his head out of the cab window. "What's going on?"

"Oh, hallo, Ben, is that you? Well, you'll think I'm barmy, but someone seems to have eaten the traffic lights."

Mr. Jones reflected. He backed his cab fifty yards down the Crescent again, and got out.

"Mortimer!" he shouted. "Where are you?"

"Nevermore," said a voice at ground level in the dark behind him. Although he had been expecting something of the kind, Mr. Jones jumped. Then he turned around and saw Mortimer, with his eyes shining in the light of the streetlamps, walking slowly along by the hedge, peering in at all the front gates of the houses in turn. He was on the wrong side of the road, so it was likely that he would have passed clean by Number Six and gone on goodness knows where. Mr. Jones picked him up.

"I probably ought to turn you over to the police for eating the traffic lights and causing an obstruction," he said severely. "But Arabel's ill in the hospital, so I'm going to take you to see her. And you'd better behave yourself."

"Kaaaark," said Mortimer. Mr. Jones was not absolutely encouraged by the way he said it.

He went home, because he had not yet packed up the nightdresses, tea bags, and digestive mints. While he was finding these things, Mortimer wandered into the kitchen and saw the large dish of spaghetti that Mr. Jones had cooked for his supper.

Mortimer looked at it thoughtfully. He loved spaghetti as a rule, but just at present he was so full of bananas that he felt unable to eat anything else.

"Kaaaark," he said sadly.

He wanted to make some use of the spaghetti, however, since he wasn't able to eat it, so he looked around for a container. When allowed to do so, Mortimer greatly enjoyed packing spaghetti into jam jars or sponge bags or old yogurt pots.

He had just disposed of the spaghetti when Mr. Jones came back with the mints and nightdresses, took a box of tea bags from the kitchen cupboard, dropped all these things into the tartan shopping bag, put on his overcoat again, and picked up Mortimer.

By now it was quite late in the evening, but Mr. Jones supposed that it would be all right to go to the hospital, although it was after proper visiting hours, because the doctor had told him to bring Mortimer.

He drove his taxi to Rumbury Central, parked it outside, and walked in with Mortimer on his shoulder.

Mortimer was amazed by the hospital. It had been built about a hundred years ago, of stone, and was huge, like a prison. Several of its corridors were about a mile long, and the echoes from even the smallest sound, even things outside in the street, were so loud that many patients believed the nurses and doctors were allowed to drive cars along the passages, although this was not actually the case.

Mr. Jones went up to the fourth floor in a huge creaking lift—at which Mortimer said, "Kaaark," because it reminded him of the lift in Rumbury Tube Station—and then walked along miles of passage until he found Balaclava Ward. There was nobody outside the door to ask if he might go in, so he stood on tiptoe and peered through two round glass holes like portholes in the double doors. He could see a double row of white-covered beds and, some distance off, Mrs. Jones, sitting by one of them. He caught her eye and waved. She made signs that he was to wait until the sister—who wore a white pie-frill cap and sat at a desk near the door—noticed him and let him in.

Mr. Jones nodded.

He stuck his hands in his pockets and prepared to wait quietly.

But he didn't wait quietly. Instead, he let out a

series of such earsplitting yells that patients shot bolt
upright in their beds all over that wing of the hospital, porters rammed their trolleys into doors, nurses
dropped trays of instruments, ambulances started up
outside and rushed away, doctors jabbed themselves
with syringes, and Mortimer flew straight into the air
and flapped distractedly round and round, shouting,
"Nevermore, nevermore, nevermore!"

Mr. Jones fainted dead away on the floor.

Sister Bridget Hagerty came rushing out of the
ward. She was small and black-haired and freckled;
her eyes were as blue as blue scouring powder; when
she gave orders for a thing to be done it was done
fast. But everybody liked her.

"What in the name of goodness is going on
here?" she cried.

Dr. Antonio arrived. He was in charge of that
wing of the hospital at night and had just come on
duty. He was not the same doctor who had told Mrs.
Jones to have Mortimer brought. In fact, Dr. Antonio
couldn't stand birds. He had been frightened by a
tame cockatoo at the age of three, in his pram; ever
since then the sight of any bird larger than a blue tit
brought him out in a rash.

He came out in a rash now, bright scarlet, at the
sight of Mortimer.

"It's obvious what's going on!" he said. "That

beady-eyed brute has attacked this poor fellow. Palgrave! Where are you?"

Palgrave was the orderly, who had just been bringing the doctor a cup of instant coffee. He came running along the corridor at the doctor's shout.

"Palgrave, get that bird out of here."

"Yes, sir, right away," said Palgrave, and he opened a window and threw the cup of coffee all over Mortimer, who was still circling around overhead, wondering what had come over Mr. Jones.

Mortimer didn't care for coffee, unless it was very sweet, and his feelings were hurt; he flew out of the window.

"Doctor, there's something very funny about this man," said Sister Bridget, who was kneeling by Mr. Jones. "Why do you suppose his hands are all covered with spaghetti in cheese sauce?"

"Perhaps he's an emergency burn case," suggested the doctor. "Perhaps he couldn't find anything else and used the spaghetti as a burn dressing. We had better take him along to the Casualty Department."

"But his pockets seem to be full of spaghetti, too," said Sister Bridget.

"Perhaps he was on his way to visit some Italian friends," said Dr. Antonio. "Perhaps he *is* Italian. *Parla Italiano?*" he shouted hopefully into Mr. Jones's ear.

Mr. Jones groaned.

"Parla Italiano?" said the doctor again.

Mr. Jones, who had flown over Italy as a Spitfire pilot in World War II, said feebly, "Have we crashed? Where's my gunner? Where's my navigator?"

"A mental case," said Dr. Antonio. "Speaks English, hands covered in spaghetti, asks for his navigator. Without doubt, a mental case. Palgrave, fetch a straitjacket."

Luckily at that moment Mrs. Jones walked out,

wondering what had become of Ben. When she saw him lying on the ground, his hands covered in spaghetti, she let out a cry.

"Oh, Ben, dear! Whatever has been going on?"

"Do you know this man?" asked Sister Bridget.

"He's my husband. What's happened to him?"

"He seems to have fainted," said the sister.

Mr. Jones came to a bit more. "Worms," he said faintly. "Worms in my pocket. It was the shock—"

"Oh my goodness gracious, I should think so, whatever next," cried his wife. "Worms in your pockets, how did they come to be there then?"

"It wasn't worms, it was spaghetti," said the sister, helping Mr. Jones to sit up and fanning him with the straitjacket which Palgrave had just brought. "Could you fetch a cup of tea, please, Palgrave? How did you come to have your pockets full of spaghetti, Mr. Jones?"

"Instant coffee, instant straitjacket, instant tea," grumbled Palgrave, stomping off.

"Spaghetti? Oh, that'll have been Mortimer, bless his naughty ways," said Mrs. Jones. "Last time I left him alone with a bowl of spaghetti for five minutes he packed it all in among my Shetland knitting wool. Arabel's friends were asking where she got her spaghetti–Fair Isle sweater—*Ben!* Where *is* Mortimer?"

Mr. Jones struggled to his feet and drank the cup of tea Palgrave handed to him.

"Mortimer? He was here just now. Have you seen a raven?" he asked Palgrave.

"Raven? Big black bird? I chucked him out the window with a cup of Whizzcaff up his tail feathers," said Palgrave.

"Oh no!" wailed Mrs. Jones. "Dr. Plantagenet said a sight of Mortimer was the one thing that might make Arabel feel better."

She looked beseechingly at the sister. Sister Bridget looked at Palgrave. Palgrave looked at Dr. Antonio, who looked at his feet.

"Better go outside and start looking for him and quick about it," said the sister.

"Instant coffee, instant straitjacket, instant tea, instant raven," grumbled Palgrave, and went out through the fire door onto the fire escape.

Where, all this time, *was* Mortimer?

Outside the windows of Balaclava Ward there was a balcony that ran right along. There Mortimer sat in the dark, thinking gloomy thoughts.

He was quite tired. It had been a long, exciting day: first of all the roller skating, then the bananas, then the chimney, then the soot, then the two-mile walk from Auntie Brenda's house to Rainwater Crescent. Then the traffic lights.

Mortimer longed for his cozy white shiny enamel bread bin; his feet hurt and his tail feathers felt fidgety from the Whizzcaff, and his wings were sore where Lindy, Cindy, and Mindy had pulled them, and he wanted to go to sleep very badly.

But also he had a kind of feeling that Arabel was somewhere not far off, and he wanted to see her very badly, too.

Limping a little, muttering and croaking under his breath, he started going sideways along the parapet of the balcony, looking through each window as he came to it.

Just inside the third window there was a bed which at first looked as if there was nobody in it; the person was so very small, and lying so very flat, not moving at all.

Mortimer flopped across from the parapet to the windowsill and looked through the glass, his black eyes as bright and sharp as pencil points. "Kaaaark!" he said.

The person in the bed didn't stir.

Mortimer tapped on the closed window with his beak.

Nobody came to let him in. Sister Bridget was talking to Mr. and Mrs. Jones at the other end of the ward, a long way off. All the other patients were asleep. Nobody heard Mortimer.

Down below, on the ground, Dr. Antonio and Palgrave, with torches and butterfly nets, were hunting for Mortimer in the hospital garden. They weren't finding him.

Mortimer sighed. Then he spread his wings and hoisted himself into the air. He flew along the row of windows tapping each in turn. They were all shut. Fresh air came into the ward through small round ventilators; no use to Mortimer.

When he had been all along one side of the ward and back along the other side, Mortimer flew up over the roof. Here he found a chimney and perched on it.

The chimney had a familiar sooty smell. Mortimer stuck his head down inside and listened. Then he sniffed. Then he listened again. Then he tapped with his beak on the chimney pot. Then he came to a quick decision and dived headfirst down the chimney.

Luckily for Mortimer they had given up using stoves to heat Rumbury Central Hospital. They had electric radiators instead. But the stoves were still there, because nobody had time to remove them, and anyway it would make too much mess.

In the middle of Balaclava Ward there was a big blue stove, shiny, with a big black stovepipe leading down to it, and two doors that opened in front, with shiny little mica panes in them so that you could see the fire behind them when it was lighted.

Mortimer came clattering down the chimney head-

first and landed inside the stove, with two pounds of
clinker and a bit of soot—though nothing like so
much as had been in Auntie Brenda's chimney, because this one had been regularly swept.

He made the most amazing noise inside the
chimney. Several of the patients woke up and thought
it was Santa Claus.

Sister Bridget came running.

Mortimer was trying to open the doors, but he couldn't. He did get his head out through one of the mica panes, though, and glared at Sister Bridget as she came up to him.

"Is that your bird?" Sister Bridget asked Mrs. Jones.

"Oh good gracious, bless my precious soul, *yes*, however did he get in there, the naughty wretch. Oh, dear Sister Bridget, do get him out of there quick, please, I'm so anxious about Arabel, she doesn't seem to take notice of *anything*."

Sister Bridget undid the screw that kept the stove doors shut. When she opened the doors, out swung Mortimer, with his head still stuck through one of the panes. Sister Bridget grabbed him around the middle. She didn't hurt him, but she held him tight while she worked his head backward through the hole he had made.

Then she held him up and had a look at him.

"Did you ever in all your born days see a bird in such a filthy state?" she said. "That bird is going to have a bath before he goes anywhere near your daughter or my name's not Moira Bridget Hagerty."

"Nevermore," said Mortimer.

"Oh please be quick then," sobbed Mrs. Jones. "I think he's her only hope, I truly do! Oh my goodness, I'm sorry I ever said a word against his pecking, munching ways and if Arabel gets better he can undo every bath towel and hearthrug we have in the house!"

Sister Bridget carried Mortimer into a white-tiled room called the Sluice and there she suddenly put him under a jet of warm soapy water. Mortimer let out a yell and struggled as if he were being barbecued. Sister Bridget took no notice at all. She held him in the jet of water until every speck of soot had run off him. Then she clapped a hair dryer over him which was so powerful that in two minutes flat he was bone-dry and his feathers were sticking out all around like the rays of the sun.

By this time he was in a bad temper. And when Sister Bridget lifted the dryer off him he sidled toward her as if he would have liked to give her a good peck. But Sister Bridget stood no nonsense, from nurses, from doctors, or from ravens.

"Behave yourself now!" she said sharply to Mortimer, and she picked him up around his black middle and took him over and put him on Arabel's bedside locker.

"Arabel dearie," said Mrs. Jones, "here's Mortimer come to see how you are getting on."

Arabel didn't answer. She lay very white and quiet with her eyes shut.

Mr. Jones gave a gulp and blew his nose.

Mortimer looked at Arabel. He looked at her for a long, long time. He sat still on the polished wooden locker staring at her. Arabel didn't move. Mortimer didn't move either. But two tears ran down, one on either side of his bill.

Then he hopped down onto Arabel's pillow. He hopped close beside her head, and listened at her left ear. He listened for a long time. Then he went around to the other side and listened at her right ear.

Then he croaked a little, gently, to himself, and made a tiny scratching noise with his claws on the pillow. Then he waited.

There was a pause. Then, very slowly, Arabel

rolled over onto her stomach. She turned her face a little and opened one eye, so that she could just see Mortimer with it.

"Hullo, Mortimer," she whispered.

Nobody breathed much.

Then she turned her head the other way, so that she could see Mrs. Jones.

"Mortimer's tired out. He wants his bread bin," she whispered.

"Oh, Ben—quick!" Mrs. Jones gulped.

Mr. Jones went very quickly and quietly out of the ward. He didn't like to run until he was on the landing. Then he fairly hurled himself down the hospital stairs and rushed out to his taxi.

"Bird's found; going to get bread bin," he panted to Palgrave and Dr. Antonio, who were standing scratching their heads, wondering where to search next.

Mr. Jones drove home as fast as he dared. He ran into the kitchen at Number Six, Rainwater Crescent, tipped the loaves of farmhouse, whole meal, and currant malt, and a bag of rice buns out of the bread bin onto the floor, and carried the bin out to the taxi. He hadn't even switched the engine off.

When he got back to the hospital everyone was in exactly the same position as when he had left, except that Palgrave was there with a pot of cocoa, and Dr. Antonio with a bright scarlet rash.

Arabel had shut her eyes again, but when her father whispered, "Here's the bread bin, dearie," she opened them.

"Put it on the bed," she whispered, and curled herself into a *C* shape.

Mr. Jones put the bread bin into the middle of the *C*. It had two enamel handles, one on each side. Mortimer stepped down from Arabel's pillow and climbed slowly, by means of the handle, onto the rim of the bin. Then he jumped down inside. Then he stuck his head under his wing and went to sleep.

Arabel reached out a hand from under the bed-clothes and took hold of the enamel handle. Then, holding the handle, she, too, went to sleep, quietly and peacefully.

"Would you look at that, now?" said Sister Bridget.

"Oh my gracious, now I suppose we'll have to keep the bread in the coal scuttle," said Mrs. Jones. Mr. Jones sat down beside her and they went on sitting by Arabel all night.

Sister Bridget took Dr. Antonio away to put something on his rash.

Palgrave drank the pot of cocoa, as nobody else seemed to want any.

In the morning Arabel's cheeks were pink and her eyes were bright. Mortimer was as black as ever, still asleep, with his head under his wing.

"She'll do now," said Dr. Plantagenet, coming to look at her. "But don't let her out in the rain again for a long time."

"She'll just have to stay indoors, then," said Mrs. Jones, "for I don't think it's *ever* going to stop raining."

But just then it did stop, and a watery blink of sun peered through the hospital window. Arabel was too weak to speak much yet, but she pointed to it and smiled a little.

Mr. Jones leaned over and gave his daughter a kiss, then he went off to drive his taxi and buy a new coal scuttle.

Mrs. Jones settled down with her knitting by Arabel's bed.

Mortimer went on sleeping in the bread bin with his head tucked under his wing.

The Escaped Black Mamba
and Other Things

It was not long after Mortimer the raven took up residence with the Jones family, at Number Six, Rainwater Crescent, Rumbury Town, London, N.W. 3½, that Mr. and Mrs. Jones received an invitation to the Furriers' Freewheeling Ball, at the Assembly Rooms, Rumbury Town.

"What is a freewheeling ball?" asked Arabel.

She was eating her breakfast. Mortimer the raven was sitting on her shoulder and peering down into her boiled egg to see if there were any diamonds in it. Mortimer was going through a phase of hoping to find diamonds everywhere.

There were no diamonds in the egg.

"A freewheeling ball," said Mr. Jones, gloomily putting on his taxi-driving overcoat, "is six hours on your feet after a long hard day, with your best suit throttling you, and nothing to eat but potato chips."

"Kaark," said Mortimer. He loved potato chips almost as much as diamonds.

Arabel imagined them all in their best clothes, pushing a huge freewheeling ball round and round the Assembly Rooms.

"You will go, won't you?" she said anxiously. "Then Chris Cross can come to babysit."

"I daresay we'll have to," said Mr. Jones, looking at the hopeful faces of his wife and daughter. "But mind! If Chris comes he's not to play his guitar after eleven at night. Last time we had trouble from the neighbors right up to the High Street."

He kissed his family good-bye and went off to drive his taxi.

As he shut the front door Mortimer the raven fell headfirst into Arabel's boiled egg.

"Oh my good gracious, Arabel," said Mrs. Jones, "why in the name of mystery can't you teach that dratted bird to *balance* I don't know. I'm sure you'd think a creature with wings would have the sense not to lean forward till he topples over, *look* at the mess, if I lived to ninety and ended my days in Pernambuco I doubt if I'd see anything to equal it."

"Nevermore," said Mortimer. As his head was still inside the boiled egg, the word came out muffled.

"Do they have boiled eggs in Pernambuco?" said Arabel.

"How should I know?" said Mrs. Jones crossly, clearing away the breakfast things. "For gracious' sake, Arabel, put that bird in the bath and run the tap on him. How I shall ever get to the office in time I can't imagine."

Mrs. Jones now worked at Nuggett & Coke, the coal order office. Arabel and Mortimer loved stopping in to see her there; Arabel liked the beautiful blazing fire that always burned in a shiny red stove, and Mortimer liked the sample lumps of coal in pink bowls on the counter.

Arabel didn't put Mortimer in the bath. She put him, boiled egg and all, into her red wagon and pulled him into the garden. Mortimer never walked if he could ride. And he never flew at all.

"That bird's got an egg on his head," said the milkman, leaving two bottles of Jersey, two of orange juice, a dairy cake, a dozen ham-flavored eggs, and three yogurts (rum, brandy, and Worcestershire sauce).

"Why shouldn't he, if he wants to?" said Arabel.

The milkman had no answer to this, so he went on up the street.

Presently the egg fell off, Granny came in to look

after Arabel and Mortimer, and Mrs. Jones went to work.

Granny made pancakes for lunch and Mortimer helped toss. Granny did not entirely approve of this, but Arabel said probably there were no pancakes where Mortimer came from and he should have a chance to learn about them.

Anyway, they got the kitchen floor scrubbed long before Mrs. Jones came home.

On the night of the Furriers' Freewheeling Ball Chris Cross came in to babysit.

Arabel loved Chris. He was not very old, still doing his A levels at Rumbury Comprehensive, and he had first-rate ideas about how to pass the evening when he came to the Joneses'. He thought of something new each time. Last time they had made a Midsummer Pudding, using everything in the kitchen. Also he sang and played beautiful tunes on his guitar.

"Arabel's to go to bed at half past eight," said Mr. Jones.

"What about Mortimer?" said Chris. He and Mortimer had not met before; they took a careful look at one another.

"He goes when he likes. But he is *not* to get into the fridge or into the bathroom cupboard," said Mrs.

Jones, putting on her coat. She was wearing a pink satin dress with beads on it.

"Not too noisy on that guitar, now," said Mr. Jones.

"I brought my trumpet, too; I'll play that instead if you like," said Chris.

Mr. Jones said the guitar would be better.

"And no trumpet after eight, *definitely*," he said.

"Supper's in the kitchen," said Mrs. Jones. "Mince pies and cheese patties and tomatoes and chips."

"Kaark," said Mortimer.

"What flavor chips?" said Arabel.

"Sardine."

Mr. and Mrs. Jones went off in his taxi and Chris at once began singing a lullaby.

"Morning moon, trespassing down over my
  skylight's shoulder,
Who asked you in, to doodle across my
  deep-seated dream?
—Basso bluebells chiming to ice as the night
  grows colder—
Be off! Toboggan away on your bothering
  beam!"

Arabel loved listening to Chris sing. She stuck her finger in her mouth and sat quite quiet. Mortimer

perched in the coal scuttle, listening, too. He had never heard anybody play the guitar before. He began to get overexcited; he jumped up and down in the coal scuttle about a hundred times, opening and shutting his wings and shouting, "Nevermore!"

"Doesn't he like it?" said Chris.

"Oh yes, he *does*," said Arabel. "It's just that he's not used to it."

"Maybe we'd better dress up as Vikings and play hide-and-seek."

"How do we dress as Vikings?"

"In towels and helmets."

Arabel used a saucepan as a helmet and Chris used the pressure cooker.

"A towel's going to be too big for Mortimer," she said.

"He can have a face towel. And a sardine can as a helmet."

Arabel thought a frozen orange-juice can would be a better shape.

Mortimer was very amazed at his Viking costume. They fastened his face towel on with safety pins. When it was his turn to hide he climbed into the bathroom cupboard (they had opened it to get the towels out). While he was in the cupboard he had a good hunt for diamonds, tearing some sheets and pillowcases and leaving coaly footprints on Mrs. Jones's Terylene lawn nightdress. He did not discover any diamonds. His helmet fell off.

"The cupboard is terribly hot," said Arabel, when she found Mortimer. (She had guessed where to look, as he was so fond of the bathroom cupboard.) "My goodness, Ma went out leaving the immersion heater switched on; the hot-water tank is almost boiling. I had better switch it off." She did so.

"Ma *will* be pleased that I thought of doing that," she said.

When it was Chris's turn to hide, it took a very long time to find him, as he had packed himself tightly into the laundry basket and pulled the lid down over his head. He had a book in his pocket and meant to read, but went to sleep instead.

Arabel hunted for Chris all over the house.

Mortimer, meanwhile, had another idea. He was wondering if there might be any diamonds in the hole inside Chris's guitar. He went off to have a look, leaving Arabel to hunt for Chris by herself. She found her right gumboot, which had been missing for a week, she found a chocolate egg left over from last Easter, she found three pancakes that Mortimer had hidden inside the record player and forgotten, but she did not find Chris.

However, Mortimer was annoyed to discover that Chris, who never took chances with his guitar, had placed it and the trumpet on top of the broom closet. Since Mortimer never flew, the guitar was out of his reach.

He looked angrily around the kitchen, with his bright eyes that were as black as privet berries.

The ironing board stood not far away.

Mortimer was very strong. He began shoving the ironing board across the kitchen floor. After five minutes he had it up against the cupboard.

Meanwhile, Arabel was still hunting for Chris. She looked in the hat and coat closet under the stairs. There she found a plastic spade left over from Littlehampton last summer, and two bottles of champagne, which Mr. Jones had hidden there as a Christmas surprise for Mrs. Jones. No Chris.

Mortimer considered, looking at the ironing board.

Then he knocked over the garbage bucket, tipping out the garbage, got onto a chair, holding the bucket in one claw, and climbed from the chair onto the ironing board. He put the bucket on the ironing board, upside down, and got on top of it.

He still could not quite reach the top of the broom cupboard.

Arabel looked for Chris under all the beds. She did not find him, but she found one of her blue bed-socks, a ginger biscuit, last Sunday paper's color supplement, and a tooth she had lost three weeks ago.

Mortimer got down from the garbage bucket and found a square cheese grater. He made his way back and put the cheese grater on top of the bucket; then he clambered carefully up and stood tip-claw on the cheese grater's rim.

Still he could not quite reach the top of the cupboard.

Arabel looked for Chris under the bath. She did not find him, but she found all the pearl-handled knives and forks, Mrs. Jones's wedding-present fruit set, that had disappeared shortly after Mortimer came to live in the house. It had been thought that a burglar had taken them.

"Ma *will* be pleased," Arabel said. She carried all the knives and forks to the kitchen in a fold of her Viking towel.

When she reached the kitchen the first thing she saw was Mortimer.

He had jammed a milk bottle into the cheese grater, which was on top of the bucket, which was upside down on the ironing board, and he was now carefully climbing up so as to stand on top of the milk-bottle.

"Oh, Mortimer," said Arabel.

Mortimer turned his head at the sound of her voice.

A lot of things happened at once. The bucket fell off the ironing board, which fell over, the cheese grater fell off the bucket, the milk bottle (full of best Jersey milk) fell out of the cheese grater with Mortimer holding on to it.

The noise woke Chris, curled up asleep inside the laundry basket, and he came to see what was happening.

Arabel had a brush and dustpan and was sweeping up bits of broken glass. Mortimer was sitting by the stove looking ruffled. There were splashes of milk all over the floor and some large puddles. Quite a few other things were on the floor, too.

"It's a good thing we had two bottles of milk," Arabel said, remembering that Chris was very fond of milk.

"What happened?" said Chris, yawning.

"I think Mortimer wanted to look at your guitar."

"Nevermore," said Mortimer, but he did not sound as if he meant it.

"I'll leave the guitar there for the time," said Chris, giving Mortimer a hard look.

"Shall we have supper, as we're all in the kitchen anyway?" said Arabel.

So they had supper and Mortimer cheered up.

He was not keen on cheese patties, so Arabel got some frozen braised beef (which he was *very* keen on) out of the fridge. While she was thawing it under the hot tap Mortimer sat on the cold tap, jumping up and down with impatience and muttering, "Nevermore," under his breath. When he was too excited to wait any longer he took the packet from her, whacked a hole in the foil with his big, hard, hairy beak, and ate the braised beef in a very messy way. Arabel spread the *Evening Standard* on the floor, and some of the gravy went on that.

Then Mortimer realized, from the scrunching, that the others were eating potato chips.

He climbed onto the arm of Arabel's chair.

"Do you want some chips, Mortimer?"

Mortimer jumped up and down. His black eyes shone like the currants on sticky buns.

Arabel put a handful of chips on the table in front of him.

Mortimer began treating them as he had the pan-

cakes; he tossed each one in the air and then tried to spear it with his beak before it fell.

All things considered, he was remarkably good at this; much better than Chris and Arabel, who began trying to do it, too. But they hadn't got beaks, and had to catch the chips in their mouths.

Mortimer was spearing his forty-ninth chip when he hit the milk bottle which was standing beside Chris. It fell to the floor and broke.

"It's lucky we'd drunk half the milk already," said Arabel.

Unfortunately, Chris cut his hand while picking up bits of glass.

"Ma says you should always sweep up broken glass with a brush," said Arabel. "What's the matter, Chris?"

Chris had gone very white and quiet. Then he went green. He said, "I always faint at the sight of blood." Then he fainted, bumping against the broom cupboard as he went down. His trumpet was dislodged and fell to the floor.

"Oh dear, Mortimer," Arabel said. "It was a pity you knocked over that bottle. I wonder what we had better do now?"

She tried soaking a face towel in the spilled milk and rubbing it on Chris's forehead. Then she switched on the fan heater to warm his bare feet. Then she put a spoonful of ginger marmalade into his mouth. That made him blink. Mortimer shouted, "Nevermore!" in his ear. He blinked again and sat up.

"What happened?" he said.

"You fainted," said Arabel.

"I always faint at the sight of blood." He looked down at his cut finger.

"Well, don't faint again," said Arabel. "Here, put this around it." She tore a strip from the face towel and bandaged Chris's finger with it.

He stood up, swaying a little.

"You ought to have brandy to make you better," said Arabel. "But Pa keeps the brandy in his taxi, in case of lady passengers turning faint."

"I'd rather have milk," said Chris.

However, both bottles of milk were now broken.

"There's a milk machine by the dairy in the High Street," Chris said. "I'll go and get some more."

"Ma said you were not to go out and leave me," said Arabel. "I'll come, too."

"It's your bedtime."

"No it isn't, not for five minutes by the kitchen clock. We'd better go right away."

Arabel decided that she did not need a coat, and she was still wearing her Viking costume, which was a very thick orange towel, and her saucepan helmet. She took the front-door key from the nail on the dresser.

"Come on then," said Chris.

"I wonder if Mortimer had better come, too? Ma doesn't like him left alone in the house."

When they looked around for Mortimer, who had been very quiet for a few minutes, they found that he had got himself jammed inside Chris's trumpet, face towel and all. They pulled at his feet, which stuck out, but they could not shift him.

"He must have been looking for diamonds," said Arabel. "We had better not wait. We can get him out when we come back; I expect if we trickle in a little cooking oil it will loosen him."

"Thanks!" said Chris. "Am I supposed to play my trumpet when it's full of sunflower oil?"

"Well, it would be better than sump oil," said Arabel.

Luckily, Chris's trumpet had a hole in it (he had bought it for ten shillings at a junk shop and stuck a Band-Aid over the hole when he played), so Mortimer was not likely to suffocate. Arabel put him in her red wagon, with his feet sticking out of the trumpet, and they walked up to the top of Rainwater Crescent, where it joins Rumbury High Street.

It was a dark, windy night. Nobody was about, though they could hear music and voices coming from the youth club at the other end of the street.

When they reached the milk machine by the dairy Chris found that he had nothing but pennies and a fifty-penny piece. The machine would take nothing but fivepenny pieces.

"We could get change at the youth club," said

Arabel. "It would be silly to go back without any milk now we've come so far."

They walked toward the youth club. There was an arcade leading up to it, with fruit machines on each side. Arabel had a penny of her own, so she put it in one of the fruit machines. Some little red balls lighted up and rushed about and clanked and shot through holes and bounced on levers and all of a sudden a whole shower of pennies and fivepenny pieces and tenpenny and fiftypenny pieces shot out into the metal cup on the machine's front and a big sign lighted up that said, "You are the winner. You are the next best thing to a millionaire! Why not have another go?"

Mortimer was amazed. As it happened, he had been looking that way, through the hole in the trumpet, when all this happened.

"Now we don't need to change your fiftypenny piece, which is good," said Arabel. "We can go back to the milk machine."

So they turned around. Several people had noticed Arabel winning the money, because the machine made such a commotion. A couple of men looked at Mortimer. Nothing could be seen of him but his stomach, the tips of his wings, and his two feet sticking out.

The men got into a Citroen car, which was parked illegally just outside, and followed along the street.

Chris put a fivepenny piece in the slot of the milk-vending machine. Wheels whirred and levers went up and down inside; presently a carton of milk came thumping down into the space in the middle.

This time Mortimer had been watching very intently through his hole. When the carton of milk came into view he said "Kaark!" several times and began to jump up and down, trumpet and all.

"I think he'd like you to put in another fivepenny piece," Arabel said.

This time when Chris put in the coin for some reason the machine went wild and shot out six cartons of milk.

"My goodness," said Arabel. "We haven't paid for all that. You'd better put in five more fivepenny pieces."

"I don't know," said Chris. "It isn't our fault if the machine goes crazy."

"We can easily afford to. We've got ten pounds and forty-three pence. I've been counting."

So Chris put in five more coins. Nothing happened. The milk machine was tired out.

While Chris and Arabel were piling the seven cartons of milk in the red wagon beside Mortimer, one of the two men in the Citroen car (which was now parked a little way off) whispered to the other, "Reckon that's him all right, Bill, don't you?"

The other man nodded.

"The boss is going to be pretty pleased about this, hey, Sid? We'll snatch him back farther along, where it's quiet."

"Guess they've got him in that trumpet for a disguise."

"Loopy sort of disguise," muttered Bill, letting off the hand brake and letting the car roll slowly along the street.

Arabel, Chris, and Mortimer were now on their way home. But Mortimer did not want to go home just yet. He had never seen automatic machines before; he thought they were the most interesting things he had ever come across, and he wanted to know all about them.

As the red wagon passed Gaskett and Dent, the big garage on the corner, Mortimer looked out through the hole in his trumpet and said, "Kaark!" Sometimes when he spoke inside the trumpet he accidentally blew quite a loud note. It happened this time, and the Citroen car swerved across the road.

"What does Mortimer want?" said Chris.

"I think he would like us to put a coin in that machine."

"All-night kerosene? What would we want kerosene for?"

"We could use it instead of cooking oil for getting Mortimer out of the trumpet."

"Oh, very well," said Chris. He put in a tenpenny

piece and got a carton of kerosene. Mortimer would have liked him to do it again, but Chris thought one lot of kerosene was enough.

"There's a bread machine at the baker's," Arabel said.

"It *must* be past your bedtime by now."

"Well, we don't *know* that," Arabel said, "because we none of us have watches. Mortimer *would* so like to get a loaf from the bread machine."

But at the baker's they had a disappointment. The bread machine was out of order. A sign said so.

"Nevermore," said Mortimer, inside the trumpet.

"Poor thing, he does sound a bit sorry for himself in there," said Chris. "Tell you what, as we've come so far, we might as well go up to the tube station. There's lots of machines up there."

"Oh *yes!*" said Arabel.

Rumbury Tube Station had recently been modernized inside, after an accident to its lift and escalators. A whole lot of new automatic machines had been installed in the station entrance. One sold hot milk, soup, hot chocolate, or coffee black or regular, with or without sugar. Another had apples, pears, or bananas. Another had sandwiches or meat pies. Another had paperback books. Another would polish your shoes. Another would take a photograph of you looking as if you had seen a ghost. Another would massage the soles of your feet. Another would say a cheering poem and hold your hand while it did so. Another would print your name and address on a little tin disk. Another would tell your weight and horoscope. Another would blow your nose for you on a clean tissue, if you stuck the nose into a slot and, as well as that, give you a vitamin C tablet and two mentholated throat lozenges, all for fivepence.

There was also a useful machine which would give you change for all the rest.

Arabel's uncle Arthur was the stationmaster. "Arr," he used to say, "there's that variety of machines at Rumbury Toob now, a man wouldn't need kith nor kin nor wife nor fambly; he could just pass his life in the station and they wondrous machines'd do all he needed. Even his wash he could get done next door at the Washeteria; all they won't do for you is sleep."

Uncle Arthur never needed anyone to do *his* sleeping for him. He was asleep now, with his head pillowed on a pile of fifteen-penny tickets, snoring like a municipal garbage truck.

Mortimer looked around at all the automatic machines with their little glass windows and things all bright behind them; his eyes sparkled through the hole in the trumpet like buttons on patent-leather boots.

"Where shall we start?" said Arabel.

Sid and Bill left their Citroen parked illegally

outside on a double yellow line and strolled up to the station entrance. They stood leaning against the wall, looking in.

"Bit public here," said Bill. Sid nodded.

It was at this moment in the Rumbury Town Assembly Rooms, in the middle of the Furriers' Freewheeling Ball, that Mrs. Jones suddenly left her partner (Mr. Finney the fishmonger), rushed up to Mr. Jones, who was gloomily eating potato chips at the buffet, grabbed his lapel, and said, "Ben! I've just remembered! I left the immersion heater on! Oh my stars, do you suppose the tank will burst and all our sheets and towels be ruined and what about Arabel and Mortimer and that boy Chris, though I daresay he can take care of himself, do you suppose they'll be scalded, oh my goodness gracious, what a fool I am, what shall we do?"

"It won't burst," said Mr. Jones, "but it'll be costing us a bundle. I'll phone up home and tell Chris to switch it off."

"I'll come to the phone with you," said Mrs. Jones, "and make sure Arabel's in bed and everything's all right."

There was a wall telephone in the lobby. Mr. Jones dialed his home number but nobody answered. The bell rang and rang.

"Funny," he said. "Maybe I got the wrong number. I'll try again."

He tried again. Still no answer.

"Oh, Ben!" said Mrs. Jones fearfully. "What could have happened? Could the house have burned down?"

"Don't be silly, Martha. How could the phone ring if the house had burned down? Maybe it's a crossed line. I'll get the exchange to call them."

He got the exchange. But all they could say was that nobody was answering on Rumbury oh one one oh.

"Oh, Ben! What could have happened? Do you think the boiler did burst? Or perhaps there's been a

gas escape and they're all lying unconscious or masked gunmen are holding them up and they aren't allowed to phone or there was something deadly in those cheese patties and they're in agony trying to crawl down the stairs or maybe there's a black mamba escaped from the zoo coiled around the banisters and they can't get by. I've always *said* it was silly to have the phone halfway up the stairs, oh my gracious, we must go home directly!"

"Don't be silly. We haven't *got* gas, Martha, so how could it escape?"

"From the zoo!" cried Mrs. Jones, frantically waving her cloakroom ticket at the lady who was knitting by the counter. "Oh, please, dear, find my coat quick, there's a love, for a deadly masked mamba has escaped from the gasworks and it's got into the cheese patties and if we don't get home directly there won't be one of them alive to tell the tale!"

"What tale?" said the cloakroom lady, rather puzzled, and she was even more puzzled when she looked at the ticket which said, "Clean and retexture one pink satin dress."

"This one, this one then," said Mrs. Jones, distractedly fishing out another ticket which said, "Rumbury Borough Library Nonfiction." "That one, that black coat with the sparkling butterfly brooch on the collar, oh please hurry, or I shall pass out with palpitations, I know I shall."

"Why did Mr. and Mrs. Jones go off so quick?" asked the cloakroom lady's cousin, Mrs. Finney, presently, bringing her some chips and a glass of sparkling cider.

"Oh, Grace, it's awful! One of those deadly cheese mambas has escaped from the telephone exchange and there's gunmen going after it because its breath is like a poison gas and it's in Mr. Jones's house coiled around the boiler and everybody's dead and someone just rang from the zoo to tell them to come home."

"My lawks. I'd better tell my hubby, he's a great friend of poor Mr. Jones. Perce, Percy, just listen to this: a deadly mamba has escaped from Mr. Jones's house and it's in the telephone exchange with a gun and they're trying to gas it out with deadly cheese and all Mr. Jones's family are unconscious inside the boiler and his house is burned down."

"Cripes," said Mr. Finney, who was a member of the auxiliary fire brigade. "I'd best be off, they'll be wanting all the lads at that rate." He went toward the entrance, muttering, "I wonder why they got inside the boiler?"

"Take your gas mask!" his wife screeched after him.

Most of the men at the Furriers' Ball were glad of the excuse to stream after Mr. Finney, and their wives followed, all agog to see what was happening at Number Six, Rainwater Crescent. A procession of cars started away from the Assembly Rooms, in pursuit of Mr. Jones's taxi.

Meanwhile, Mr. and Mrs. Jones had arrived at Number Six.

"At least the *house* is still standing," cried Mrs. Jones. "Open the door, Ben, do, I couldn't if I was to be turned to a nutmeg on the spot, my hand's all of a tremble and my saint pancreas is going round and round like a spin dryer."

Mr. Jones unlocked the door and they hurried in.

"Arabel," called Mrs. Jones. "Arabel, dearie,

where are you? It's Mum and Dad come home to save you!"

No answer.

Mrs. Jones rushed to the kitchen, where the light was on.

"Oh my dear cats alive! *Ben! Look!* Oh, whatever has been going on? Broken glass everywhere—blood—milk—towels—what's that guitar doing up on top of the cupboard?—cheese grater on the floor, chips everywhere, pressure cooker in the laundry basket—a whole *gang* of mambas must have been in!"

Even Mr. Jones was obliged to admit that it looked as if there had been a struggle.

"I'd best call the police," he said unhappily, when he had been all over the house, and made sure that neither Arabel, Mortimer, nor Chris were anywhere in it. "There's been something funny going on in the bathroom cupboard, too; one thing, the intruders seem to have had the sense to turn off the immersion heater."

"Oh, how can you talk about immersion heaters when my child's been gagged and tied up in a lot of sheets and towels," lamented Mrs. Jones. "Kidnapped, that's what they've been, by a gang of those deadly gorillas that live in the river Jordan. Oh, Ben! We'll never set eyes on them again. My little Arabel! And Mortimer! To think I'll never see him digging for diamonds in the coal scuttle anymore!"

"Oh, come, Martha, things may not be as bad as that," said Mr. Jones doubtfully. "Let's see what the police say." He went to the phone.

"Send back a lock of hair in a matchbox, they will," wept Mrs. Jones. "Or a claw, maybe! Heart of gold that bird had at bottom; just a rough diamond with feathers on, he was, Many's the time I've seen him look at me as though he'd have *liked* to say a kind word if his nature would have let him."

"I want the police," said Mr. Jones into the telephone.

But at that moment the police came through the front door, which was open.

It was Sergeant Pike, who had met Mr. Jones the month before when Mortimer helped to catch some bank robbers. With the sergeant there were two constables.

"Evening, Mr. J.," said the sergeant. "Someone up the town reported you've an escaped snake in the house, is that right?"

"Snake? Who said anything about a snake?" Mr. Jones was puzzled. "No, it's my daughter, and our raven Mortimer, and the babysitter who seem to have been overpowered and kidnapped, Sergeant. You can see there's been quite a fight here. Look at this blood on the floor."

"Carried off to Swanee Arabia they've been by a band of gorillas," sobbed Mrs. Jones.

"That's yuman blood on the floor, that is," said one of the constables, as if no one had noticed it before.

"You can see there's been a struggle. Someone tore a strip off that towel."

"For a gag, likely."

"The guitar got tossed up on top of the cupboard in the roughhouse."

"The ironing board got kicked over in the ruckus."

"Someone bashed someone's head with a milk bottle."

"And then the other bloke took and bashed him back with another bottle."

"And collared him when he was down and scraped him with the cheese grater."

"That'll be Grievous Bodily Harm, shouldn't wonder."

"Cheese grater," said the sergeant thoughtfully. "Wasn't there something about some poisoned cheese patties?"

Just at that moment the fire engine drew up outside.

"Can we help?" said Mr. Finney who, with his mates, had got into auxiliary fire uniform.

"I dunno," said the sergeant. "Why are you all wearing gas masks?"

"Someone said a tank full of deadly mambas had exploded and there was gas about."

Now all the ladies from the Furriers' Ball turned up.

"We've brought hot tea and blankets," cried Mrs. Finney. "Where's the injured persons?"

"Strewth," said the sergeant. "How am I expected to get on, with all this shower?"

People swarmed over the house, looking at the mess.

"Do you find you can get your sink *really* clean with Dizz, dear?" said Mrs. Finney to Mrs. Jones. "I always find it stains."

"Fancy you still having those old-fashioned plastic curtains in your kitchen. Give it ever such an old-world look, don't they? *My* hubby *made* me change to shades, ever so much more modern and labor-saving, he said."

"Haven't you ever thought of getting a sink garbage disposal unit, dear?"

"I have lost my beloved daughter and my greatly esteemed raven," said Mrs. Jones with dignity, "and I should be obliged if you would leave me alone with my trouble."

"Yes, why don't you ladies go and have a hunt up and down the street, see if you can lay eyes on the little girl," said the sergeant, "or one of these here pistol-packing mambas I hear talk of. Be off, buzz along, that's right, let's have a bit of peace and quiet around here, can we?"

"Suppose we meet the mambas, what shall we do?"

"It isn't mambas, it's gorillas," wailed Mrs. Jones.

"Do not attempt to engage them in combat but inform the police," said Sergeant Pike. "If you patrol the High Street in half dozens I daresay you'll be safe enough."

He shoved the reluctant ladies out of the house.

"What about us?" said Mr. Finney, hopefully peering about for something to bash with his fireman's ax. In his gas mask he looked like some creature that had climbed up out of the deep, deep sea.

"You cruise up and down the High Street in your engine and assist the ladies in their inquiries," instructed Sergeant Pike and shoved him out, too. "Now, Mr. and Mrs. Jones, if you'll just accompany me up to the station and make a statement, perhaps this case can proceed in a proper and orderly manner."

"Why go up to the tube station? Oh my stars, why can't we make a statement here when all the time my Arabel's lying bound and gagged on some railway line in the desert with all the Arabian knights of the Round Table ready to chop her in half if she moves hand or foot?"

Police Constables Smith and Brown, who had been searching the house, came to report.

"Someone's been incarcerated in the bathroom cupboard," P. C. Smith said. "There's an empty can of orange juice there, also a ginger biscuit, a chocolate egg, and three battered pancakes."

"Ah," said Sergeant Pike, "that proves it was a carefully planned and premeditated job. The intruder must have been hiding in the bathroom cupboard before you left for the ball, Mr. Jones, just waiting till you were out of the house."

"He must have been ever so small then," wept Mrs. Jones, "for *I* never saw him when I turned the heater on for Arabel's bath. Oh my goodness, it must have been one of those wicked fiendish little dwarfs capable of superhuman strength like Mr. Quilp in

The Old Curiosity Shop or the hunchback of the Aswan Dam."

"Let's get up to the station, for Pete's sake," said Sergeant Pike, who began to feel he was losing his grip on the case. "Do you want to come in the police car or will you follow in your taxi?"

"We'll follow," said Mr. Jones. After the police had left he carefully locked the house, and he and Mrs. Jones followed in the taxi. But they got left behind almost at once because whenever Mrs. Jones laid eyes on a group of searching ladies she put her head out of the window and shouted, "It's not gorillas after all, it's those wicked little dwarf Arabian knights with curved swords that go round cutting cushions in half in old curiosity shops."

Meanwhile, up at Rumbury Station, Arabel, Mortimer, and Chris had been having a wonderful time. Mortimer, jumping up and down in frantic excitement inside his trumpet, had watched while they put coins into every single machine, one by one. In the red wagon, as well as seven cartons of milk and the kerosene, they now had a packet of gumdrops, two bars of chocolate, one of nuts and raisins, some cigarettes, a ham sandwich, four empty cups (one chocolate, one milk, one coffee, one soup), an apple, a pear, a banana, a copy of a paperback book called *Death in the Desert*, a make-it-yourself record with Chris singing his song about the moon, a meat pie, an

identity disk with Mortimer's name and address
printed on it, a photograph of Arabel with Mortimer
in his trumpet on her shoulder, a card saying that
Chris weighed ten stone and would have six children,
a vitamin C tablet, and two mentholated throat
lozenges. Also, Arabel had had her nose blown and
Mortimer his feet massaged, which astonished him
very much indeed.

"That's all," said Arabel regretfully when they
had put the mentholated throat lozenges into the
empty cup that had held tomato soup. "Could we
start again?"

"No, we ought to go home," said Chris. "It must be your bedtime by now."

"We could wake Uncle Arthur and ask him the time in case it isn't."

"No, don't, he looks so peaceful. Come on, we can make some hot chocolate when we get back."

They pulled Mortimer out of the tube station in his wagon and started down the hill. The two men who had been waiting outside got back into their Citroen car and followed.

But Mortimer, when he found that the evening's entertainment was finished, became very despondent. He began to grumble inside the trumpet, and to mutter, and flap his wings, or try to, and kick the carton of kerosene, and shout, "Nevermore!" in a loud angry voice.

"He's upset because *he* didn't have a chance to put a coin in a machine," said Arabel.

"He shouldn't have got inside my trumpet."

"If we could only get it off him," said Arabel, "we could turn down Lykewake Lane and go home that way. There's a draper's shop that has a machine outside that you put fivepence in and it sews a button on while you wait."

"Who wants a button sewn on?"

"Mortimer might like one on his face towel."

"Oh, all right."

So they turned down Lykewake Lane (just missing one of the posses of ladies and the fire engine cruising along the High Street) and the two men followed them in their Citroen car.

When they came to the draper's shop, which was called Cotton & Button, Arabel said, "Mortimer. Will you stop shouting 'Nevermore' and listen. We are going to pull the trumpet off you, if we can, and then you can put fivepence in this machine for it to sew on a button."

Silence from inside the trumpet while Mortimer thought about this.

"Do you think we really ought to pour kerosene on him?" said Chris. "It might be bad for him. And it will make my trumpet smell terrible."

"Well," said Arabel, "if you don't think we ought, Pa told me there's an Italian grocer's shop in Highgate that has an olive-oil machine."

"I'm not walking all the way over to Highgate."

"In that case we'll have to use kerosene," said Arabel. "Mortimer, we are going to turn you upside down and pour a little kerosene into the trumpet so as to loosen you and pull you out. Will you please try not to struggle?"

Silence.

Arabel picked up the trumpet and turned it upside down. Chris picked up the kerosene container.

At this moment the two men who had been fol-

lowing got out of their Citroen car and came quietly
up beside them. Both were holding guns.

"Hold it, sonny," said the one called Sid. "That's
a valuable bird you've got in that trumpet. Don't you
go pouring kerosene down it or you might spoil him."

"We know he's valuable," said Arabel. "He's my
raven, Mortimer."

"How are we going to get him out if we don't pour
kerosene?" said Chris.

"Why are you holding guns?" said Arabel. "You look rather silly."

"That bird's no raven. That bird is a valuable mynah bird, the property of Slick Sim Symington, the Soho property millionaire. That bird was kidnapped last week by a rival gang—by a rival establishment—and it is our intention to get possession of him again. So pass him over."

"Pass over Mortimer?" said Arabel. "Not likely! Why he's my very own raven, he loves me, and he certainly isn't a miner bird, whatever they are."

"We'll soon see about that," said Bill. Putting his gun down in the red wagon he grabbed hold of the trumpet with both hands while Sid, putting down *his* gun, grabbed Mortimer's feet.

There was a short, sharp struggle during which it was hard to see what was going on. Then the scene cleared, to show Mortimer sitting on Arabel's shoulder. His face towel had come off. The trumpet was on the ground. The two men were both bleeding freely from a number of wounds.

"Nevermore," said Mortimer.

"*I'll* say it's nevermore," said Bill. "That's no mynah bird."

"What a tartar," said Sid. "Lucky he missed my jugular! You're right, miss, he's a raven, and all I can say is, I wish you joy of the nasty brute."

"Very sorry you were troubled," said Bill. "Here,

come on, Sid, let's get over to Rumbury Central *quick,* and have us some antitetanus injections before we're rolling around like the exhibits in one of those kinetic shows."

They jumped into their Citroen car and roared off, just missing the fire engine as they turned into the High Street.

"Hey," shouted Arabel. "You've left your guns behind."

But it was too late, they were gone.

"Oh well," said Arabel, "perhaps they'll call in for the guns tomorrow. Anyway, now, Mortimer, you can sew on some buttons. We've got eighteen fivepenny pieces left."

So Mortimer, jumping up and down with satisfaction and enthusiasm, put eighteen coins into the slot machine and it sewed seventeen buttons onto the face towel. (One of the coins turned out to be a five-centime piece with a hole in it.) Then they went home and let themselves in with Arabel's key. They tidied up the kitchen and the bathroom cupboard. Chris mopped the floor. Then he made a saucepan full of hot chocolate while Arabel had a bath, and he brought her a mugful in bed, and she drank it. Then she had to get out of bed again to brush her teeth. Then she went to sleep. Mortimer had already gone to sleep in the coal scuttle. He was tired out. Chris put all the cartons of milk except the one they had

used for chocolate into the fridge, with the ham sandwich, the meat pie, the gumdrops, the chocolate bars,
and the mentholated lozenges; he put the cigarettes,
apple, pear, and paperback book on the dresser, and
the kerosene outside in the shed. He ate the banana.

He did not know what to do with the guns, so he
left them in Arabel's red wagon.

Then he put his do-it-yourself record on the record
player and sat down to listen.

*"Morning moon, trespassing down over my
    skylight's shoulder,
Who asked you in, to doodle across my
    deep-seated dream?"*

At that moment the front door burst open and in
rushed Mr. and Mrs. Jones, police, firemen, and a lot
of ladies with blankets and tea.

"Arabel? Oh, where's my child?" cried Mrs.
Jones, when she saw Chris.

"Where's the gorillas?" asked Mrs. Finney.

"And the mambas?" asked Mr. Finney.

"And this here gang of dwarf Arabian hunch-
backs?" said Sergeant Pike.

"Arabel? Why, she's asleep in bed," said Chris,
puzzled. "Where else would she be? You're back
early, aren't you?"

Mrs. Jones ran up the stairs.

Sure enough, there was Arabel, asleep in bed.

"What about Mortimer?"

"He's asleep in the coal scuttle."

There was a long, long silence while everybody gazed about at the tidy kitchen.

At length Mr. Jones said, "What's that guitar doing up on top of the broom cupboard?"

"I put it up there to be out of Mortimer's reach," said Chris. "He wanted to look for diamonds inside it."

"He does do that sometimes," Mr. Jones said, nodding.

After another long silence Sergeant Pike said, "If you ask *me*, everybody in this room has been suffering from one of them mass delusions. If you ask *me*, we'd better all forget about this evening's occurrences and go home to bed."

Nobody disagreed. They all filed silently out of Mrs. Jones's kitchen and out of the house. Mr. Finney muttered, "Maybe there *was* an escape of gas and it sort of affected everybody's mind. Or maybe it was food poisoning. Those chips at the Assembly Rooms weren't very fresh."

Mr. and Mrs. Jones paid Chris his babysitting fee and he went home. Then they went to bed. They were almost as tired as Mortimer.

Next day, when Mr. Jones had gone off to drive his taxi, Mrs. Jones said to Arabel, "What's all this milk doing in the fridge, and this meat pie and ham sandwich?"

"We'd used up all the milk so we went and got some more from the automatic machine."

"Did you go out after your bedtime?"

"No, it was twenty-five past eight. We got some other things from automatic machines, too. Those cigarettes are a present for Pa, and that book is a present for you."

Mrs. Jones looked at the paperback called *Death in the Desert*. It had a picture of a person tied to a railway line.

"Thank you, dearie. I'll read it sometime when I'm not busy," she said, and put it on a high shelf of the dresser. Then she said, "Where did those toy guns come from?"

"I don't think they are toys," said Arabel. "They belong to two men, I think they were miners, who thought Mortimer was an escaped miner's bird. But they soon saw he wasn't."

"Funny," said Mrs. Jones. "But I believe I did hear they used birds in the mines. I didn't know miners had to carry guns, though. Oh well, I daresay they'll come back for them."

She put the guns on another high shelf.

For a long time after that, people in Rumbury Town talked about the evening when the deadly black mamba escaped from the gasworks.

Mrs. Jones was so pleased to have back her pearl-handled knives and forks that she forgave Arabel for the seventeen buttons sewn on and the strip torn off the face towel.

Mortimer slept in the coal scuttle for thirteen hours solid. Then he woke up and began digging for diamonds. He threw all the coal out onto the kitchen hearthrug, lump by lump.

But he did not find any diamonds in the coal scuttle.